STO

by

AUDRA GRAYSON

CHIMERA

Stolen Servant first published in 2001 by
Chimera Publishing Ltd
PO Box 152
Waterlooville
Hants
PO8 9FS

Printed and bound in Great Britain by
Omnia Books Ltd, Glasgow.

The characters and situations in this book are entirely imaginary and bear no relation to any real person or actual happening.

STOLEN SERVANT

Audra Grayson

This novel is fiction – in real life practice safe sex

By the same author

A KEPT WOMAN

Chapter One

Genetta took a long drag on her cigarette and stared out at the grim car park. Vague thoughts flitted across her mind, but it felt good to be quiet after spending all morning on the phone. Anyway, her break was almost over. She glanced down at her watch and seeing the time, dropped her cigarette onto the asphalt and stepped on it daintily with the ball of her leather-soled, cream-coloured stiletto shoe.

'Time to get back to the phones, girls,' she announced.

'Oh, Genetta, you do spoil everything,' Marie said. 'You really are such a naughty girl, telling us what to do. Especially when, as your boss, I should be the one telling you what to do. You slave drive us every time we come out for a cigarette.'

'They're bad for us, anyway, as you well know,' Genetta retorted, but she was smiling.

'Bad girls, bad cigarettes,' Marie said. She walked to the back door of the office block and turned the key in the lock. The smokers, all dressed in smart business suits, filed into the building as Marie held the door for them. Genetta passed her boss last, and as she took the single step up, she flashed another smile at her.

'I only do it to impress you,' she said.

'You only do what to impress me?' Marie asked.

'Boss the other girls.'

'But we know who the real boss is, don't we?'

'Yes…' Genetta nodded before finishing her thought.

'But you're such a fun sort, I thought perhaps I could be something like the teacher's pet. If I tried hard enough.'

'Keep trying, and you might be my pet yet.' Marie reached out, just a few inches, and her fingertips traced down Genetta's forearm as she spoke. Slowly, Genetta moved forward, turning slightly away from the contact, but her body yearned for more.

She walked into the corridor and was suddenly conscious of the way her hips swayed as she walked in her high heels. Her skirt had a small slit up the back – nothing too revealing – but would Marie think it... unprofessional? Marie, after all, always wore conservative colours, clean lines, trousers and waistcoats and soft, silky, long-sleeved blouses.

Genetta wrenched her thoughts away from Marie's wardrobe and took her place back at her desk, in front of two overlapped posters of Ibiza and Jamaica. Her phone rang immediately.

'Hello, Mowbray's Travel,' she answered upon picking up the receiver, then spun to face her computer and began typing in dates, destinations and preferred carriers.

'Why do cheap bloody people take vacations, anyway?' Genetta shouted in her friend's ear. 'Some of them wince when you tell them that a flight to Mauritius is going to cost anything at all!'

Tracey laughed, but did not answer. Genetta shrugged, grabbed her friend's hand, and headed for the dance floor.

The coloured lights spun and flashed, turning the moving bodies into shards of filmy paper in a kaleidoscope. Genetta pulled her tight, short skirt even higher up her thighs and, tilting her chin up, shut her eyes. The driving house music thumped in her chest like an animal trying to escape her shapely body.

Raising her arms above her head, Genetta danced. She bent her knees, rode down low, and moved her hips in tight circles. When Tracey bumped her arm and offered her the evening's drug of choice, Genetta refused it – the dance would give her the escape she needed.

She knew that the massive televisions covered one huge wall in the club, but in her absorption, Genetta didn't see herself appear on the first screen. The music flowed seamlessly from one song to the next, the rhythm, the throb always steady, and Genetta was transported. She felt the sweat rolling down her back as she swayed and ground and moved, then it rolled down her thighs and arms. Confined in the music's wordless world, bound by her own sensations, Genetta did not notice as the crowd thinned around her and picture after picture of herself appeared on the screens.

A low, purring voice interlaced with the beat, and it spoke words that Genetta felt herself perform, absorb and become.

'Go girl, dance. Move that body. Lift your skirt, baby, let's see what you've got. Yeah, now act like that's a man between your legs. He's on top of you, work him, slide on him.' Genetta encircled her arms in front of herself, threw her head back, and began pumping against a man she could almost feel.

The finger that ran down her exposed throat brought her to reality. She opened her eyes and found herself staring up into a stranger's face. He breached the circle that her arms made by pulling her hands apart and entered her embrace. Then he took her chin between forefinger and thumb and turned her face towards the wall.

Her own image towered there. Every camera had been

trained on her as her dance's intensity grew. Now every screen contained a portion of her body and face. Genetta faced herself, fractured at the same time that she was whole, and gigantically looming over everyone else. The picture shocked her, and she felt herself go weak for a moment in the stranger's arms.

'You are very beautiful,' he leaned down and said huskily into her ear.

'I'm glad you think so,' she said, laughing, but a bit self-conscious now. Her partner grabbed her wrist, pulled her hand to his mouth, and kissed the palm.

'You're the most beautiful woman here by far,' he said, his voice still throaty and deep. She let her fingertips rest against his lips as and after he spoke. Overall, the impression he left with her was one of masculinity. His arms held her securely, his hand clasped her wrist easily, and his chest felt hard and solid. Genetta stole another look up at him. He was not the most beautiful man she'd ever seen or met, but then, she'd had enough of those.

She dropped her head on his chest as she turned to face the screens again. Slowly, now that the show was much more tame, the cameras went back to their usual business of panning the crowd, seizing on one dancer, and giving her an opportunity to be famous for thirty seconds.

'Just how long was I up there?' Genetta lifted her face to look at her new partner again and asked.

'Long enough for everyone in this place to know who I'm with when they see us.'

She took another long look at him. There was something decidedly different about him, although in every other way, he was just a regular looking chap.

'You're tanned,' she finally said.

He smiled down at her. 'And you're observant.

'So what am I now?' His hand slid up the back of her flimsy shirt, over the strap of her bra, and rubbed across her shoulder blades.

'Very cheeky, I'd say,' Genetta murmured.

'And now?' He bent down and began running the tip of his tongue over her neck, right under her ear.

'Spot on,' she whispered. She straddled his leg and began moving up and down, but without pressing her crotch against him.

He moved his mouth to her ear. 'Are you normally this sexually forward when meeting someone for the first time, or has your dancing made you drunk?'

'I like you,' she said. 'You're bold.'

'That's not what I asked,' he said, and she knew that he would not take her deflection for an answer.

'I want you. My pussy is making me "sexually forward".'

He said no more. His hand slipped out of her shirt and he pulled her hips towards himself. Reaching around, he palmed the cheeks of her bottom and began to squeeze. Genetta groaned at the kneading and pushed her snatch hard against the firmness of his thigh. Jiggling her hips back and forth, she got her split open inside the silken thong she wore, and her clit was exposed to this unyielding grind.

They pushed against each other's hips, and Genetta felt his brazen stiffness wanting her. She swung her leg over his to stand between his thighs. Slowly, she knelt and worked her way down his torso. She gently bit the buttons of his loose-fitting white shirt. Finding a slot between two buttons, she pushed her tongue into it and teased his belly. Finally, she crouched in front of him, ran her hands up and down his strong legs, and bobbed her head up and down, as if sucking his erection. Her nose and lips bumped against his straining hard-on again and again – she knew that she was tantalising him, making his cock feel as if it were on fire.

The man grabbed her arms and pulled her to her feet. Spinning her around, he began shoving his hips against her bottom, and Genetta responded by pushing back as hard as she could. He grabbed a handful of her hair and used it as a rein, pulling her head back and arching her towards him. She shut her eyes again and grimaced at the slight pain he caused her.

Then he pulled her upright by her hair, and still holding it, began walking. Genetta had no choice but to follow his lead and move in front of him across the dance floor. He was pushing her towards a group of tables in a dark corner. She knew he wanted to finish what they'd started, right there, with her bent over and holding onto the rungs of a chair.

'No,' she protested loudly. 'Not here. I won't do it!'

'Fine, then,' he said behind her. With a tug he changed direction, and Genetta could tell they were headed for the men's room. He wanted her to straddle his cock as he sat on a toilet, but she had enough experience to know that such scenes in public could end with a gangbang and a dose of the clap. She stopped dead in her tracks.

'Oh no, I'm not doing that, either,' she said adamantly.

'So now you're backing out.'

She twisted her head around and he let go of her hair. 'I never agreed to anything in the first place,' she pointed out.

'So the mating dance out there meant nothing?'

'I'm not going to fuck you in a club, if that's what you're after.'

'Then where shall I fuck you?'

She licked her lips and looked up at him. He was aggressive. Persevering. She liked that. 'My place,' she said.

Genetta got into a black cab outside the club and sat well away from him. When he got in and began sliding quickly across the seat towards her, she pushed hard against his shoulder with the heel of her hand. 'No touching, no fondling, no molesting until we get to my place,' she insisted.

'What about foreplay?'

'There will be plenty of time for that.'

'Why not touch my dick, just for a second?'

'If I put my fist around your cock, you'll come too fast and there won't be anything left for me when we get to my flat.'

'You're a tease,' he told her

'No, I just like men, and I like to savour the pleasure,' she countered

'Are you a come slut?' he asked bluntly, taking her a little by surprise with the unexpected frankness of the question.

'I'm not sure what you mean,' she said, and he smiled a smile that turned the corners of his mouth up slowly.

'I meant,' he stated slowly, 'do you like spunk? Do you like having it shot all over your tits and rubbed in? Do you like to have a man stand in front of you and wank until he explodes all over your face and look down at you and make you thank him for it? Do you like to have a man come in your mouth, then kiss you and share his semen with you?'

Genetta paused before making her answer. She was

sexually experienced, but that was just sex – a man fingering her, mounting her, riding up and down as she struggled to get her clit against his shaft. These new suggestions were streets ahead of that.

'Do you want to do those things to me?' she asked, trying not to sound too coy.

'All that, and more,' he confirmed, looking at her cunningly.

His hand slid up his lap and she watched as he stroked himself through his jeans. He stared at her and she stared back as the lights of London framed his head, passing by the car window behind him.

The cab pulled up in front of the Victorian building where she lived and her partner passed the driver a twenty-pound note that seemed to appear from nowhere. He did not wait for change either, but got out of the cab. Genetta opened her door, and as she lowered one high-heeled shoe to the ground, he appeared and held out his hand. She delicately laid her palm against his and squeezed his hand as he helped her to stand.

She heard the cab pull away from the kerb, and looked up at her soon-to-be lover. She let him hold her gaze for a long moment. 'Perhaps we should exchange names before we go up,' he said.

'My name's Genetta.' She stopped for a moment. 'Let's just leave it at that for now, all right?'

'That's a very pretty name. Almost edible, in fact. Pleased to meet you, Genetta – my name is Jack Adams.'

'Thank you for the compliment, Jack Adams,' she said. Genetta appreciated his candour in telling her his whole name, and still holding his hand, she led him towards the steps that rose to the large front door of the building.

'My flat's at garden level,' she said softly. 'So not long

to wait now.' She let go of his hand in order to get her keys out of her small bag. He wrapped his arm around her waist and let his hand stray up to her breast.

'Mmm... firm and pert,' he whispered. 'I cannot wait to get my mouth on them.'

The key turned in the lock and she pushed the heavy front door open. He slid his hand down to the small of her back and ushered her in before him.

The entrance hall was dimly lit and silent. As the door swung shut and closed behind them, Jack shoved Genetta against the wall. He pulled her skirt up and pushed his hand between her thighs.

'Not here, someone might come,' she panted, lifting one leg up to his hip, spreading herself, making herself available to him. Impatiently he moved aside the silkiness of her scant thong. Then he pushed one finger inside her, then two, and from the easy way they glided into her pussy she knew she was completely wet and available.

Another finger followed the first two. Genetta squeezed her eyes shut and groaned against his chest as he opened her further. She heard the sound of her wetness as his hand moved inside her, and she felt her juices increase. Her wetness was flowing over his knuckles.

She opened her eyes and looked at him. His face became level with hers as he bent down in order to engulf his hand in her pussy. His eyes were open but his mouth was shut, set grimly as he concentrated on what he was doing to her. Quickly, he pulled his three fingers out and added the fourth when he slid back up into her. He kept his fingers tightly together as they pressed inexorably up into her, and then began spreading them apart.

She panicked a little; her desire wanted him to get all the way inside, but her mind was troubled by what such reckless passion might do to her. Struggling, she writhed and twisted and tried to pull away from his persistent fingers, but he grabbed her by the shoulder and held her hard against the wall, pushing ever upward into her vagina.

'No,' she gasped as he pressed his shoulder into hers and ran his free hand over her hip. He reached behind her and began kneading her bottom as he pushed his fingers ever upwards.

The pressure cleared Genetta's mind. 'Let's go inside,' she whispered, and indicated her flat door with a nod of her head.

Groaning low in his throat, he slowly pulled his hand from her, and as he straightened his back and stood in front of her, she looked up into his eyes. He was a million miles away, apparent lost in lust.

'You won't hurt me, will you?' she asked.

'No more than you want me to,' he told her.

Her hands shook as she first tried to find her keys at the bottom of her purse, and then tried to sort out the right key for her door. Jack breathed heavily but slowly behind her, and she had the feeling he was going to get angry if she did not gain control of herself.

'I'm sorry,' she whispered as she found the key, and then let it slip from her fingers and fall to the bottom of her purse again.

'Don't apologise,' he said flatly. 'Just concentrate on what you're doing.'

She did as he said and finally clasped the key. Staring at the lock, she slid the long stem into it and turned it steadily. When she heard the bolt click, she took hold of the door handle and turned it slowly. The door pushed open easily, as if it had already made the decision to let the lovers in.

Ready to walk into her flat and engage in a night of

passion, Genetta reached back to take Jack's hand. His fingers were still sticky with her juices. She tugged him, and he crossed the threshold behind her.

Once they were both inside, she dropped to her knees in front of him and began to lick the fingers that had recently pressed their way into her. Jack curled his index finger when it was in her mouth and pulled it out slowly. He stroked the outline of her full lips with his fingertip. 'Warm, serviceable mouth,' he said softly. 'I want you to unzip my jeans with them.'

She reached up and carefully pushed aside the flap of denim that hid his zip. 'No, I told you to use only your lips. Keep your hands firmly behind your back. Clasp your hands together back there.'

She glanced up at him, only to see that he was staring down at her very seriously. Genetta did exactly as he said, and when her hands were behind her back, she nuzzled at his swollen bulge with her nose and mouth. He helped her by unfastening the brass button and pulling the zip down just enough for her to catch it with her teeth. She tugged at it several times, loving the way the harsh metal felt against her lower lip as she worked.

He grunted his satisfaction at her performance and reached down to slide the zip the rest of the way to the bottom of its track. Genetta didn't want to suck him off right here, though. She wanted her sex to be full up with his broad cock, she wanted to take that first burning load in her belly, not in her mouth. So she slowly rose, and carelessly throwing her purse on the settee, took his hand again and led him through the flat to a door. 'My bed is back here,' she said invitingly. 'Should we go into my room?'

'Nothing would be better,' he replied.

Without another word, she turned around, opened the door and led him into her bedroom. Jack moved up behind her and began running his hands over her waist and hips as they walked. She reached for the wall and flicked on the light, revealing an inviting double bed. A canopy hung suspended from wires on the ceiling, but the drape was pulled away on the side of the bed. A mirror was strategically placed on the wall nearby; Genetta loved the sight of a man making love to her.

Jack grabbed her by the hips and stopped her. Then he grasped the hem of her skirt and pulled it up. She felt it rest on the high curve of her bottom and knew that both her cheeks were exposed beneath the band of folded black material. Her thong was a cranberry red, and she imagined how inviting it looked, the thin red strap nestled in the deep valley between her buttocks, then emerging at the top and burrowing beneath her crumpled skirt to join the strip of red satin that encircled her waist.

Genetta stopped at the foot of the bed and didn't turn around to face the man who was watching her from behind. Her sex was making the silky crotch of her panties very damp as she thought of him admiring her curves and fair skin. She wanted to give it all to him. Then she felt him take her rolled-up skirt in his hand, and pull her back towards him. She rubbed her bottom against his hips, and then he let her go for a brief moment and pushed down his jeans and briefs. She felt his hard-on spring forward, the head of it butting against her bottom, and sighing, Genetta moved to catch it in her cleft.

'Come here now,' he ordered gruffly, and moved her round until they stood facing the full-length mirror on her wardrobe door. 'Oh, God, yes,' she whispered. 'I want to watch you do it to me from behind.'

'Be quiet, and look at yourself,' he said. She looked at him, behind her in the mirror, and then took a glance at her own eyes. They looked dark, in spite of the room's harsh overhead light. To her, she looked ready for a really good screw.

'Tell me what you see when you look at yourself,' he demanded. 'Tell me what you *really* see.'

'I – I see a girl who's in bad need of your cock,' she answered.

'I can see that much, but I would phrase it differently. Personally, when I look at you, all I can see is a little whore.'

Genetta blinked at the disparaging name she had just been branded with, and looked away shamefully from their reflections.

'I told you to look at yourself,' he promptly reminded her.

She forced her eyes back to meet her stare once again, and as soon as she was looking into her own soul again, he continued.

'Repeat after me: I am a little whore. Say it. Go on, say, "I am a little whore".'

Mumbling, she repeated his words.

'No, that's not right. And you know it's not right.' He pulled her skirt up even higher, to her lower back, and before she could move to avoid it, he had swung and smacked her bottom. She gasped and bit her lower lip, determined not to make another sound. 'Now tell me what you are.'

'I... I'm a little whore,' she said quietly.

'And tell me why you are a little whore,' he persisted relentlessly.

'Because I want to be fucked from behind,' she

whispered breathlessly, watching him watching her.

Jack shook his head, as though disappointed with her response. 'But it's more than that, isn't it, Genetta? It's because you would like to be treated like and fucked like a dog.'

Another smack landed. This one smarted more, and Genetta flinched, rocking forward as he hit her.

'Stand still,' he snapped.

He hit her again, stinging her flesh, and she could barely stop the yelp that rose from her throat.

'You are a little whore because I said so,' he growled. 'Do you understand that, Genetta?'

'Yes, Jack,' she said earnestly, 'I do understand that.'

'You are whatever I say you are.'

'Yes, I am whatever you say I am.'

'Yes, what...?'

'Yes... sir.' Her voice was still a tentative whisper. His rough, uncompromising treatment of her and the sting in her buttocks caused tears to blur her vision. But still, somewhat surprisingly, she did not fear him. This was a game with rules – rules that she was beginning to understand with increasing clarity.

Using her hair as a lead again, he pulled her back several paces from the mirror. He put his foot in between her high heels and nudged her feet apart from the insides.

'Spread your legs,' he instructed, and when she had done so, he said, 'Bend forward and brace yourself on your thighs, just above your knees.'

Again she obeyed without question, gripped her thighs tightly, her back elegantly straight as she bent from the waist, and craned her neck so she could see herself in the mirror. He stood behind her, surveying her enticing posture.

'Now you just watch, and feel, and learn...' he said

enigmatically.

His erect penis was like an iron spike as it probed past her damp thong and pressed into her pussy. Genetta groaned her satisfaction in unison with his first long thrust and arched her back, angling her hips and bottom for him, to aid his powerful penetration. His cock sank even deeper with her movement, and he held her hips tightly, her unblemished flesh showing white where his fingers pressed like talons. She shut her eyes in delight and began grinding back and forth against him.

'I want you to watch us,' he reminded her, so she opened her eyes and focussed on the mirror just in time to see his hand release her hip, lift, swing down in an emphatic arc, and his palm connected soundly with her stinging cheek for the fourth time, causing her to squeal softly between her rhythmic pants.

'Your next infraction will result in a serious punishment,' he informed her, his rutting movements never faltering. But he was panting too now, the pleasure etched on his face, and Genetta moved lasciviously, pulling forward until just the head of his throbbing erection was buried inside her, and then slowly inching back on his length. She tightened her pussy muscles around him, trying to milk his seed from his swaying balls.

His face was strained with the effort of stopping the surge; she could see it in the mirror. She studied him closely. He stood with his hips pushed forward, letting her control the pace and angle of his cock sinking into her. He was staring down at her pussy, gliding back to swallow him, then sliding forward again. She could picture his glistening meat as her sex reluctantly let it go. Looking again at herself in the mirror, she smiled at the power she was exercising over his pleasure.

As she watched, Jack let go of her hips and pulled his shirt off, over his head. She liked his physique and, pushing her bottom up higher so she could take him deeper, she jogged her hips backwards and felt his rod press into her again. He was still worrying about his clothes, though, and she watched him as he reached down to catch at his jeans. She moved slowly forward, loving how her pussy walls grasped for his thick penis as it left her body.

Then, as she prepared to glide her wetness back over him yet again, to engulf him, she saw him pulling the belt free from the loops of his jeans. As it slid threateningly through the loops, he pulled his hips back and she lost contact with his lovely cock completely. Genetta pouted at him in the mirror.

'Ohhh... why did you go and do that?' she softly sighed.

He didn't answer, but took the roll of her skirt again and pulled her away from the wardrobe mirror. 'Get on the bed,' he said. 'I want you on the bed.'

'Do you want me on my hands and knees?' she asked.

'Stop asking questions and do what I say – just get on the bed.'

She watched for a second as he hitched up his jeans, tucking in his rigid penis. Then she stood up and sauntered the rest of the way across the room, walking in front of him. Genetta was feeling saucy – even though he was going to be in control of the night's pleasures, she already felt she was manipulating things as she wanted them. Despite him being in charge physically, she had actually been pacing their screwing, and that realisation thrilled her. The smacks he had given her just spiced things up a bit.

He sat down on the edge of the bed, the soft duvet billowing up by the sides of his thighs. Genetta, standing in front of him, watched, waiting breathlessly for his next move.

'Turn around,' he said, and without hesitation, she did as he ordered.

Her only regret was that she could no longer see herself in the large mirror on the other side of the bed. But Jack clearly noticed the lack of perspective she had and read her thoughts, and before he set the next part of his plan into motion, he stood and moved to her dressing table against the opposite wall, and he adjusted it and tilted the oval mirror until he could see her reflection in it, and she could see her reflection in it.

When he sat back down on the bed he took both her elbows and pulled her arms back. 'Bend them,' he demanded.

She did so, but the position felt awkward. She giggled a little nervously, but he then slipped his belt around her upper arms, just above her elbows, and with one sharp tug that made her gasp and thrust her breasts out provocatively, he snapped the loop quickly shut and she felt him securing it tightly with another couple of aggressive tugs.

The tension on her shoulders grew harsh as he finished the job. Her elbows were drawn painfully close together, so much so that her shoulder blades felt as if they were rubbing against each other. When she looked at herself in the dressing table mirror, she saw the effect that her posture had on her breasts; they were straining against the tight material of her blouse and showing every detail of her lacy bra.

He stood up and moved around her, blocking the view of her reflection, and Genetta began to grow uncomfortable under his searing gaze. She sensed he was not seeing her as a woman any more, or even as a person. Bound this way, she had turned into a helpless, captive creature he could toy with and savour at his leisure without fear of her getting away.

Slowly, an expression of avarice on his face, he reached forward and popped open her blouse buttons. They slid easily out of their confines, the silky material relinquishing its hold on them with the slightest help that he gave.

He put his hands over her breasts, still neatly and tantalisingly encased in lace, and leaned back just a little as if to look at them and judge their beauty from a distance. Genetta trembled a little as he did so, but ever so slightly, she leaned the firm yet soft weight of her breasts into Jack's cupping and very gently squeezing palms and fingers.

He responded with a low chuckle and by circling her nipples with the balls of his thumbs. And then his chuckle changed to a low hum of gratification in his throat as they grew harder under his touch. She pressed herself into his palms even more, letting the mounds of her flesh mould into his hands. He squeezed her breasts and kept circling her nipples through the lace of her bra.

Then he pushed her back a little and slid his hands down to her ribs. He made as if to encircle her with his thumbs and fingers, and then let his hands stray down over her waist. She thrilled to his slow, calculating touch; the gentle way he caressed her skin.

Then sliding his hands excruciatingly slowly back up her torso, he pushed at the under-swell of her delicate lacy bra-cups. They moved up, deepening her cleavage and pinching a little of her breasts between their tight lower band and her flesh, and Jack ran his fingertips over the trapped skin.

Throwing her head back, she sighed, transported by the first bare contact of her breasts and his hands. Decadently, she ran her tongue over her upper lip as he continued pushing her bra up over her breasts, until they sprang free and the soft material became nothing more than a band running across their curvaceous upper slopes. His thumbs began circling her exposed nipples then, and she groaned when he pinched them both between thumb and knuckle.

He bent down and kissed a trail from the hollow of her throat up to her chin. His lips grazed and nuzzled at her warm skin, and she relished his tenderness, especially enjoying the contrast with the way he had given her a stinging bottom. The slight stubble on his chin scraped against her delicate throat, again in contrast with the softness of his kisses.

Tentatively, he kissed back along her jaw line and touched her earlobe with the tip of his tongue. She let her head loll to the side, laying bare even more of her neck and throat to his attention.

And he took the hint and began kissing downwards in a line, back behind the natural fall of her hair. Her knees grew weak and she nearly swooned in his arms as he drew a mouthful of her flesh between his teeth and sucked at it, delicately, before releasing it.

He moved his hands from her breasts to her waist and reached behind her to grasp her wrists. She pressed herself against his bare chest and stomach, feeling her breasts flatten warmly against him. He kissed downwards another millimetre, or so it seemed, and sucked at her neck again. Genetta moaned and rubbed more earnestly against his chest. Behind her back, her fingers reached to clasp his, and in response he slid his hands down into hers, and she held them tightly as he nibbled at her some more.

When his lips reached the collar of her loose blouse, he stopped his kissing and suckling. He pushed his hips against her belly, and she felt his cock raging to get inside her again.

'Please... do it,' she whispered hoarsely.

He moved aside just an inch or two, enough to push his erection against her hip. Her skirt still hung down a little at her front, although still rucked up as it was at the back, and Genetta yearned for him to tug it off completely, take her thong with it, and fuck her pussy once more.

But instead he placed a thumb under her chin, and tilted her face upwards. Their lips met again and his tongue pressed into her mouth, possessing it. She kissed him ferociously, opening herself, pushing her tongue against his. Their merging heat melted them together, and she became lost in the wet warmth, no longer able to tell where he started and where she stopped.

His hand was between her legs again as he pulled his mouth away from her lips. He slid his fingers across the moist silk barrier of her panties, watching her gasp with tormented pleasure, then hooked his thumbs in the waistband and pulled down; down to her knees, then he knelt in front of her and slipped her panties over the heels of her shoes, and gingerly, she obeyed his unspoken command and stepped out of them, one shapely thigh and then the other braced against his shoulders to aid her balance.

He dropped the flimsy piece of damp material aside, but did not stand up. Instead, still kneeling, with a seductive whisper of material against flesh he eased her skirt up her thighs and tucked the hem into the waistband.

She looked over his head at her reflection. She was a

dishevelled mess, but she looked to be in, even to her own misty eyes, an incredible state of horny abandon and longing.

But then she gasped again and her attention was drawn emphatically back to the kneeling man, as he cupped her buttocks, pressed his face tightly in against her fragrant crotch, and his tongue flickered out against clit, giving it a good, long, and very skilful lick. As her hips rolled and a guttural groan escaped her tongue-moistened and slightly parted lips, he pulled away and lifted his face. Genetta gazed down at him, silently begging him to continue.

'Now to kiss you properly,' he said, and pressed his mouth back against her engorged sex mound, inhaling her essence deeply through flared nostrils.

He licked her clit over and over again. The rhythm was not fast enough to threaten a climax, but it felt heavenly enough to make her beg for more, bending her knees very slightly to help him. She longed to grab his head, to entwine her fingers in his hair and pull him against her pussy and ride on his upturned face. But her hands were secured well behind her back, stayed by her bound arms, the belt cinching them tightly so all she could do was yearn for more pleasure.

He played adroitly with her nub and sex lips until she was at the end of her sexual tether. 'Please, Jack, I need more,' she begged, panting heavily, her breasts rising and falling as she inhaled and exhaled heavily, her fingers moving agitatedly against the hands that still cupped and gripped her buttocks, holding her steady so his mouth could devour her succulent pussy unhindered. 'Please, give me more... make me come... I want you to fuck me... *Jack, please...*' Maybe using his name would manipulate him; turn him on even more and make him want to move quickly to the next stage of her seduction.

And something like that seemed to happened.

He stood up and lightly ran his tongue over her lips. She could smell her juices on him, and she flicked out her own tongue to taste her humid wetness on his mouth and chin before he pulled away.

She looked up at his eyes as his glance darted over his shoulder, and then she sighed disappointedly as he let go of her and went back to her dressing table, opened one of the two small top drawers, and took out one of her bras.

It was crimson and very sexily lacy, completely see-through. Genetta was thankful that perhaps he would loosen and remove the belt from her throbbing arms and make her put on the bra, for what reason she could not fathom, but she was wrong.

He was twisting it tightly as he approached, and when he was close again, he put the twisted material against her lips and pressed. 'Mmnngg!' she managed incoherently, but as her lips parted he swiftly stretched the material between them and her teeth. Quickly he tied the ends together, tight at the back of her head, and she stood there, gagged, with her arms still tied securely behind her back.

The enormity of the realisation that she could not call out to anyone, made her begin to cry. 'Stop your snivelling,' he muttered, as he pushed his jeans and pants down and sat on the edge of the bed. 'Nothing bad is going to happen to you. I told you I wouldn't hurt you. But you're a whore, Genetta. You like to play rough, don't you?'

She felt him tug at the belt that harnessed her arms, so she took a step backwards and tumbled down onto his lap. He grabbed the belt firmly and loosened it off a little, her elbows eased apart a little by the action, and she let out her breath gratefully at the release that a few inches gave.

His fingers grasped the bra tied around her face and he pulled it and the belt towards him. She grimaced at the burning sensation in her muscles as her elbows and shoulder blades were pulled taut again.

Then he clutched her rucked-up skirt and using both hands, pushed her up a bit. She lifted her bottom and felt the tumid head of his phallus pressing against her. Without any hints or leads on his part, she jounced back a little, got his erection where they both wanted it, and sank down.

Jack grunted against her shoulder and pushed at the belt so she bent down more from the waist. Then, using both handles available to him – the belt and bra in one hand, her skirt in the other – he began to glide her up and down on his shaft.

Any control she once might have had over his pleasure was gone now completely. Jack's fists pushed against her when he wanted her pussy to slide up his hard cock, and when he wanted to impale her, he dragged her back and down again.

It was all she could do to keep her balance. The leather soles of her shoes slipped on the carpet every time he rocked her. She was half-standing, half-sitting, her feet pigeon-toed, slipping, her shoulders aching and burning, her long hair trapped to her face by the crimson gag, sticking to her neck, her cheeks and her forehead, her bra cutting into the upper slopes of her breasts, perspiration rolling down her chest and back, and still he continued to screw her greedily.

His grip tightened on her straps, he stopped pushing

her up, and instead he held her bottom tight against his groin and pushed hard, up and into her. Instinctively she held herself at the right angle and height above him, and he pumped his hips up and back again and again.

With a groan, he pulled her down against him one last time, his thighs beneath hers, and stabbed up to meet her. She gasped behind her gag, desperate for breath and freedom. He pulled her straps back towards himself tightly and she felt his legs and stomach tense, and her head drooped forward as he grit his teeth and shot his hot load into her.

Quickly, Jack undid the belt that held her arms together, then he pulled her back onto the bed and helped her to lie down. When he stood, he slipped off his clothes and gently tugged at hers, removing them for her. Feeling weary and replete, Genetta moved her limbs and let him undress her.

Then they lay together. She sprawled, her body enjoying its release from the bondage. Jack relaxed on his side, his elbow propped on two plush pillows and his head on his hand.

'You seem to be very experienced,' she said, her voice still husky from the excitement and use.

'I should say I am very experienced, yes,' he mused. 'And with a delicious submissive like you, very enthusiastic too.'

'Mmm, enthusiastic.' She smiled contentedly to herself, mulling his words over, and relaxed in his embrace. 'And did you enjoy being experienced and enthusiastic with me?'

'What do you think?' he asked rhetorically.

His head slipped languidly off his hand and rested on the pillow beside hers, and he reached out to play idly with her hair for a moment.

She turned to look at him, knowing he was not expecting an answer. 'Your accent seems to slip occasionally,' she observed, in a tone as soft as the smile that still played about her lips. 'Every now and then you sound like an American, or perhaps a Canadian. Are you either?'

'Yes,' he said, clipping the word short, and no further information about the relative stranger was forthcoming.

So Genetta carefully pried a bit further.

'All right, let's say that you're located somewhere on the other side of the big pond,' she probed. 'So what do you do over there?'

'I'm in media, working on both sides of the Atlantic,' he said, and then mentioned the name of a broadcasting company she had never heard of, but she was gratified to see a smile playing about his lips.

'You're not a broadcaster, are you?' she persisted, wanting to know more about the man. 'If you are, I've certainly never seen you before.'

'Do you listen to very much radio?' he asked, hinting at a clue.

'Sometimes at work,' she said. 'But I have to admit that I always switch stations when something serious comes on.'

'Well then, there you have it. That's why you've never heard me. I usually report on world economics and financial issues. You know; stock markets, recessions, things like that.'

'Oh no, you'll never catch me listening to those spots,' she said, shaking her head and smiling playfully.

He chuckled. 'That's all right; not everybody can be interested in multi-nationals and the Euro.

'Is it my turn to ask you a question now?' he added.

'Go on then, if you must.'

'Do you do this sort of thing very much?' he asked bluntly.

'"This sort of thing", as in…'

'"This sort of thing" as in picking up strange men in public places and bringing them home to engage in wild and debauched sex,' he elaborated.

'Oh, that "this sort of thing".' Genetta giggled mischievously and threw her head back to expose her slender white throat. 'Right, well, let me see now.' She frowned and tapped her chin as though deep in thought. 'Yes, I suppose I do pick up strange men in public places and bring them home, but never has the sex been as wild and debauched as it was just now.'

'So at least I'm different in one respect, anyway.'

'Mm… the most important respect,' she purred, her eyes sparkling.

He smiled at her blatant compliment on his sexual prowess. 'Have you ever thought about this kind of bedroom play before?' he asked. You seem… not experienced necessarily, but certainly well suited to taking part in something like this.'

'No, I can't say that I've ever really thought about it too deeply…' her voice trailed off as she answered.

'Are you telling me the truth, Genetta?' he asked, as if he already knew the answer to his question.

'No, not really,' she admitted, 'I suppose.' She hesitated before saying more, but Jack was waiting patiently. And certainly, she thought, this was a man who might understand what she had dreamt of.

So she took a breath and dived in.

'The – the fact is,' she started, a little uncertainly, 'that many times I've thought about being kidnapped. I've fantasised about being made to feel helpless and out of control. I've fantasised about my fate being in someone else's hands, of being taken away, and of being made to do things with different men... and women.'

'So you dream about being used and abused indiscriminately by strangers – abductors, even.' He pondered her admission for a few moments. 'How very interesting.'

She reached out to slap him playfully, but he grabbed her wrist and glared at her. 'None of that kind of behaviour, Genetta,' he snapped, his mood seeming to change in an instant. 'You will always be on the receiving end – and you'd do well to remember that.'

She was taken aback by his sudden change from playmate to master. 'I'm sorry,' she whispered as his fingers tightened around her shapely wrist, nearly causing her pain. 'I'm so sorry, sir,' she added.

'You learn easily, to your credit, Genetta,' he said, releasing her. 'And I'm going to want to teach you much more later. But for now, let's rest.'

He rolled away from her, onto his other side. Genetta turned her head and pushed the pillow out of her way so she might see her bedfellow's back more clearly. His volatility troubled her, but she had no doubt she'd done the right thing in bringing him back to her flat, even though she clearly had a lot to learn.

Chapter Two

Genetta kept her eyes closed when she slowly awoke, turning onto her back, reluctant to leave the night before. As she surfaced, her mind replayed images of herself as her latest lover took her from behind in front of the wardrobe mirror, her body bent at the waist, her breasts pressing out against the straining confines of her bra as they hung down. Then her drowsy mind glossed forward, to being bound and used, her body glistening with a rosy hue of perspiration as Jack Adams shoved her up and down on his stiff cock.

She sighed and rolled over, longing to press her breasts and stomach against his strong back, and longing to spoon her thighs tight against the backs of his. She felt sure he'd have the stamina and desire to start again from where they'd left off.

But when Genetta sleepily opened her eyes, she did not see Jack Adams lying beside her. She reached out quickly to feel under the sheets, over the mattress, but it was cold. Either he was an early riser, or he was…

No, she told herself sternly, he would not have left so easily after a night like the one they'd had. She climbed out of bed, slipped into her silk robe, and walked quickly through her flat, hoping to find him in the lounge, or the kitchen, or the bathroom.

But he wasn't there. He wasn't anywhere.

She put her hands on her hips and huffed. 'Bastard,' she said aloud, then turned and padded back towards her bedroom. But as she crossed behind the settee something on one of the cushions caught her eye and made her stop in her tracks. There lay her purse, but what was a little disconcerting, was that the clasp undone. She'd thrown it there last night, she thought… didn't she? And it must have opened then.

Her palms grew clammy and she balled her hands into fists, suddenly feeling extremely vulnerable. Her stomach churned and felt as if an icy hand was gripping it.

Forcing herself to move, she stepped gingerly around the side of the settee before panic took over. With a gasp she threw herself down next to her purse, scooped it up and began rifling through it.

Her wallet was there, she heard her keys jingle, and she turned the purse upside down and dumped everything onto the cushion.

Her hands were shaking as she opened her wallet, but she forced her fingers to brush over each important element. The bankcard was there, her credit card was safe, all the cash was accounted for. Recklessly she unzipped the cache to find the three twenty-pound notes she kept for an emergency, and indeed, they were there too.

She glanced over the mess on the settee – some receipts, odds and ends of make-up, a folded hairbrush and some barrettes, the usual assortment of coins that found its way to the bottom of her purse – everything seemed to be there and all right.

So how had the clasp come undone? Maybe the bag just landed awkwardly and it popped open, and had been laying that way all night.

Relieved at finding an answer to the would-be mystery, Genetta leaned back against the couch for a moment. It was a fleeting feeling of relaxation, though, and her initial grumpiness at the disappearance of Jack Adams returned. She looked around for any sign that he had ever even been in her flat with her.

She went through to the kitchen and put the kettle on, then moped around waiting for it to boil. Maybe he left a note or something, she thought. Maybe he had to get up early to report on some groundbreaking news, and left her his number. But as she paced she found nothing on any of the doors, nothing on the mirror in the loo, nothing discernable in her bedroom.

She glanced at the mess still on the settee from her purse, but went back to the kitchen to pour the boiled water over the teabag in the mug she'd put out. Coming back through to return to the toilet, she sighed and sidetracked around the side of the couch, scooped up her purse's guts and shovelled them back into it. Then off to the bathroom she went.

The toothpaste globbed out of the tube and onto the bristles of her toothbrush. Genetta glared at it, still angry with Mr Jack Adams, and ferociously stuck the brush into her mouth. In the back of her mind she wanted to get rid of the taste of him – any trace of him.

When the clear, minty flavour had suffused her head and her teeth and lips were covered in froth, Genetta glanced up at herself in the mirror. Looking into her own eyes, after the memories of last night and what Jack had made her confide in him, made her uncomfortable for a moment. But she forced herself to meet her own gaze head-on, to account for the fact that she'd fully taken part in what went on and had welcomed it. Just because he was gone now did not mean that she had to be ashamed of enjoying herself with him as much as she had.

When she looked into her eyes boldly, her soul felt absolved. She bent her head to spit the toothpaste into the basin, and then looked back up. Then and only then, as she slowly dabbed the towel across her lips, did the realisation dawn.

Her address book was missing from her purse!

'Genetta, I can't believe it!' Tracey exclaimed when they saw each other in the office first thing on Monday morning. 'There's no way he'd take your address book and ignore your money!'

'I only had about seventy quid left, and he didn't seem like the sort who'd worry about that amount of cash. But what would he want with my addresses? Is he going to supplement his own little black book with the names of all my girlfriends?'

Genetta laughed along with Tracey, but her insouciant tone barely covered the fact that she had been uneasy all weekend.

Uneasy enough, in fact, to stay at home.

She had not done her weekly shop, she had not visited any of her friends – and she had taken the phone off the hook. In the front of her address book, she remembered having written *Genetta Macleod*, along with her phone number and address. Now Jack Adams – or whoever he was – knew her surname and how to reach her from anywhere.

These thoughts must have made themselves apparent on Genetta's face, for Tracey looked at her carefully and said, 'Are you quite all right? I mean, if you're really worried about this bastard and the fact that he took your address book, anybody could be in danger. Any one of us, not just you.'

‘Any one of us could what?’ Marie asked. Her head appeared above the partition of Tracey’s cubicle. She sounded incredulous, as if she had overheard the entire conversation and just could not take it onboard.

Genetta glanced at Tracey meaningfully, then said, ‘All right, Marie, it’s a bit upsetting to rehash once again, but I will for the last time. It was on Friday night. I went clubbing and met this American at a club. Tracey was with me, she’s seen him—’

‘What happened, Gen?’ Marie interrupted. She quickly came around the cubicle, her professional semblance replaced by one of pure, apparently sincere concern.

‘Not what you’re thinking, Marie, really,’ Genetta said, reaching out to pat her boss’s arm. ‘He didn’t assault me, nothing like that. In fact, he and I had a rather nice time, I thought, and he fell asleep at my flat. But when I got up on Saturday morning he was gone and so was my address book.’

Marie blinked in disbelief, and then furrowed her brow quizzically. ‘Have you alerted everyone in the book?’ she asked.

‘Oh, Marie, that would be all my relations, my friends I had who’ve since moved to Spain and the Florida Keys, people from just about every job I’ve ever had, just about all the girls in this office – the list goes on, and that doesn’t even chip off the smallest tip of the iceberg. I’ve got professional contacts in there, an old dance instructor, my telly repairman, everything.’

‘Still, I think it’s only responsible of you to try to reconstruct the book and track people down,’ Marie insisted. ‘You should let them know that this questionable person has their info and knows of their connection to you. You have no idea what might happen, Genetta. He might ring up all of the Macleod's in your book and make his way with them, saying that he's a good friend of yours and you told him to call them.'

'Well, thanks, Marie,' Tracey chimed in. 'We just about had her convinced that it was all right, that he did it on a lark, since he didn't take her money or her credit card. And he seemed all right to me at the club.'

'You only saw him for two minutes,' Genetta muttered miserably.

'All right, only two minutes, but you liked him well enough to take him home alone,' Tracey pointed out. 'He couldn't have been all bad.'

Genetta did not get a chance to answer whether he was all bad or pretty good.

'Doesn't bode well, Gen,' Marie broke in, shaking her head sagely. 'You can hope for the best, but in the meantime, if I were you, I'd take steps to prevent the worst.'

'What can he do, really?' Tracey asked. 'Ring people up; perhaps show up at their front doors? I think anybody would be wary of something like that happening, some man calling and saying, "Hello, I'm friends with Genetta and she sent me along."'

'One never knows,' Marie said, sticking to her guns.

Genetta paused in thought before she said, 'No, you're right, Marie; one never knows,' in quiet agreement.

'You know he's American or Canadian, and you know he goes by the name of Jack Adams—' Tracey began to say.

'He *goes* by the name of Jack Adams – you suspect that isn't his real one?' Marie asked, incredulous again.

'Don't look at me like I've lost my mind,' Genetta said angrily. 'He told me his name was Jack Adams, he said he worked for some American based international broadcasting company – and I took him at face value. We'd already had sex together, and I really didn't see him as the sort of snake who would lie to me. That's what I thought, anyway,' she added ruefully.

'So if he had plans at the outset to rifle through my purse and take whatever interested him, he wasn't going to give me any real idea of his name, was he?'

'Genetta, take my advice,' Marie said. 'Contact friends and family in that book of yours. If you like we can talk after work – I'll do my best to help you jot down the names of everybody you need to call.'

When she had walked away, Genetta rolled her eyes at Tracey. 'Great – wonder if she'll let me make all those calls on company time, from these phones?'

Tracey smiled, but it was thin-lipped. 'Maybe she's right, Gen. Certainly it's something you might consider doing. I hadn't thought about it that way, but if you hadn't told me that this man had my personal info and knew how to contact me, I'd be quite upset with you.'

'How upset do you think my mum's going to be when she learns how he got hold of her address?'

Tracey shrugged and wheeled her chair forward, out of Genetta's sight.

A few minutes of strained silence went by, and then finally Genetta made her decision and said, 'Fine, Trace, I'll do it. Maybe I'll ask Marie if she was serious about helping me jar my memory loose.' To herself, she grumbled about her dumb luck and friends' consciences. And she promised herself that on the next cigarette break she'd ask Marie…

It was the last cigarette break of the day, and Genetta still did not want to admit that she was thinking in-depth about her problem. Tracey's looks all day had been incriminating, but Marie, at least, had been friendly without pressing the issue. The fifteen minutes slid by and Genetta found herself walking back into the building just in front of her boss, as usual.

'Marie,' she said, turning her head to look over her shoulder.

'What, Gen?'

'You're right, and I'm going to track down everyone I can think of who's in my address book. It's just not on to ignore the fact that he now knows who I know.'

'Good girl,' Marie smiled. 'And do you want some help?'

'Yeah, I was wondering if you were serious when you said you'd help to jog my mind loose. It might help me to talk out loud about who's in there, starting with the obvious and working my way through by association.'

'I agree, that's a good idea.'

'Right, then. When shall we get together?'

'I think right after work would be best, considering it's been a day or so already since the deed was done.'

'All right then, after work,' Genetta agreed. 'We'll meet down at the pub on the corner, if that's all right.'

'Well really, Genetta, I'd prefer to stay in the office. There are some other things I have to take care of after we're finished.'

'Okay, after work, then.'

Time dragged by after they returned to their desks. Genetta was distracted by several things, not the least of which was what she'd say if Marie tried to get details regarding her night with the mysterious 'Jack Adams'. Surely she has to be curious, Genetta thought, then shrugged her shoulders and figured that what happened between her and 'Jack' was nobody's business but her own now, and that's exactly what she'd tell the boss if pressed.

The one-on-one time with Marie came quickly enough. The office emptied quickly after all the women collected their purses, coats and belongings and said their goodbyes. Genetta remained at her desk as Tracey stopped to trade a few pleasant words with her – at least someone was satisfied with her decision to call everyone she knew and make a fool of herself and her libido in front of them, Genetta thought.

When all had gone quiet, Marie buzzed Genetta on the phone to come through to her private office. Sighing, Genetta stood and marched along the row of cubicles to the boss's door. She knocked briefly, Marie called, 'Gen, come in,' and in she went.

Marie smiled coldly from the other side of her desk, and suddenly Genetta felt as if she were on trial for something. 'If this has turned out to be a bad time, I can go along home,' she said hastily.

'No, Genetta, this is fine. I have to say, though, after your reluctance to take me up on my offer this morning, I'm surprised that you'd want to stay now.'

'It's the right thing to do,' Genetta said. 'My friends should be told about this creep having their details.'

'It certainly is, Genetta, and they certainly should. Which is why I'm surprised you're volunteering to do it.'

'What?' Genetta wondered what her boss was getting at. 'What do you mean?'

'I mean that you're not a girl who often does the right thing,' Marie stated frankly – if somewhat unfairly. 'Leaving Jack Adams at the club would have been the perfectly right thing to do, but you didn't. You started this episode off badly, so it's somewhat surprising to see you change tacks now.'

Genetta stared in disbelief, opened her mouth to speak, and then shut it again. She turned towards the door as if to leave, but there was no way she could let Marie talk to her that way, boss or not. So she spun back around.

'You have no business speaking to me in that manner,' she said firmly. 'I didn't come in here for a lecture or a morality lesson. You offered your help to me earlier in the day, I thought to take you up on it—'

'Why?' Marie interrupted.

'Why? Because – because I thought that perhaps I needed a friend's advice to get through this. But to tell you the truth, I don't know why I stayed late after all. I know one thing for dead sure, though: I would never have stopped in here if I'd known you were going to come down on me.'

'I'd rather *go* down on you,' Marie said softly, a calculating smile playing about her lips.

'What?' Genetta was still glaring at her boss, but she laughed nervously in spite of herself.

'I'd rather go down on you than come down on you,' Marie repeated. 'And I'd rather have you go down on me after you come.'

'If – if I understand what you're saying—' Genetta began, but Marie finished for her.

'You do understand perfectly. You want it, Genetta, you know you do. And if you can be a very, very bad girl in order to give a man his pleasure, you can be a very, very good girl and help us both to get off.'

Genetta felt a tantalising ache build between her legs. Her gaze was riveted on Marie's mouth, the full, pouty lower lip coated in plum lipstick and gloss.

'But what about my responsibility to friends and family?' she blurted. 'What about the imperative of letting them know about this dodgy Jack Adams bloke?'

'You can take care of that on your own time,' Marie told her disinterestedly.

Genetta sat down on the chair across from Marie, nonplussed at what was developing. She'd never even considered that Marie – her boss – might be attracted to her... that she might be a lesbian.

As she sat and tried to get her head around what was happening, Marie stood and sauntered confidently around the desk. The dark waves of her hair cascaded around her shoulders. She wore a cunning expression, her tongue tracing the curve of her rouged upper lip. Once standing before Genetta, their knees almost touching, she leaned her bottom back on the front edge of the desk. 'I'll let you mark down this time and get paid for it in exchange for being my pet,' she purred.

Genetta looked up at her with wide bewildered eyes. 'Being your...?'

Her voice failed her as Marie reached down and began running her manicured fingertips over Genetta's knees and pressed down between them, easing them apart slightly and then gliding up her inner thigh towards the hem of her skirt. Quickly, she found the place where the stocking tops ended and the soft skin started. Genetta gasped and shivered a little when Marie's long fingernails traced a leisurely zigzag pattern from the top of her stockings to the crotch of her silk panties, but sat rigid, doing and saying nothing to repel the advances of her boss.

Marie pressed her fingertips to the elastic of Genetta's

knickers and slid her fingers beneath them. Genetta's legs parted a little more, but of their own volition this time. Marie smiled knowingly, and rubbed the lips of Genetta's pussy, caressing them gently, and then followed the curve over the hood of her clit, and massaged there, too.

Genetta moaned, caught up in the feeling of growing ever more wet, but not having her boss dip into her just yet. She loved being fingered, masturbated and teased like this, and Marie was such an expert at it. She applied just enough pressure and guile to keep Genetta's attention on what was happening between her thighs, but not quite enough to satisfy her.

'I'll make you come,' Marie said in husky tones. 'He didn't please you; he just used you as a hole for his cock. But I'm going to make sure you get to relieve your hot little pussy.'

'Mmm, yes please, Marie,' Genetta whispered, despite her confusion.

With alluring ease of movement and elegance, Marie knelt on the office carpet in front of her prey.

She eased her hands beneath Genetta's thighs to her bottom, encouraging her to slide forward a little on the chair. Then deftly, she unfastened two of the garter clasps that held Genetta's stockings. She slid her open hands around Genetta's hips, squeezing, then undid the front clasps. Genetta instinctively lifted her hips again and Marie accepted the unspoken invitation and slipped her panties down. Genetta bent her knees as Marie pulled them all the way off, and dropped them on the floor.

Genetta, acting on impulse now, lifted her legs one by one and rested the backs of her knees on Marie's shoulders and her calves on her back, drawing her boss's face in close to the wet heat. Marie made a V with her fingers and put them around Genetta's swollen lips. Then she squeezed her fingers together and began moving them quickly up and down in turn.

The sensation was very nearly unbearable for Genetta. It was better than a vibrator, desperately better, because it was so indirect. Genetta felt her clitoris, still nestled deep, growing hard under Marie's friction and touch. She groaned, needing more contact. This felt so good, though, that she did not want it to stop for a long while yet.

Marie pushed her face down into Genetta's groin and took a long lick over her mound. It was exquisite. She took another long lick, but this time stopped at the crucial point and made her tongue into a point. With that hard tip, her fingers still stroking, she drove into the slit.

She found Genetta's hot-wired button quickly. The meeting between tongue and clit sent a jolt through Genetta. Her back straightened, then arched, and she tried to bear her pussy down on Marie's face. Marie's hand held her back, though, and Genetta was forced to let her boss dictate the terms of their engagement.

She handed over control willingly. The warm velvet of Marie's mouth petted and poked at her aching nub. And still the tight constriction of Marie's fingers prevented her clit from rising to its full, engorged height.

'I want you to suck me like it's a little prick,' Genetta moaned lewdly, and upon that request Marie let her fingers loosen. The sudden release was so good; Genetta felt her pussy lips, flooded with juice, expand thankfully when the pressure was gone. They spread wide open, allowing Marie access to every millimetre of their vulnerability.

And Marie, experienced in the arts of seduction as she was, took complete advantage of it. She used both hands to pull Genetta even wider, and the tip of her tongue was now flush against the tiny knob and root of pleasure. Inside herself, Genetta marvelled at how Marie seemed to know every inch of her body so intimately. The observation didn't have time to last long, though.

Marie pulled her face away from Genetta's crotch. 'It's your turn,' she said, and grabbed Genetta's wrists and pulled her up. Genetta stood a little unsteadily, and Marie pulled her to the side of the chair. She unbuttoned her trousers and pushed them down, dragging her panties and tights with them. Her heels were kicked off with the rest of her clothing.

Genetta looked at her trim bottom and slim hips as Marie walked around the desk and bent to open a drawer. When she closed it, she held a make-up compact. Then, she swung her half-clothed body into her opulent chair and put one of her feet up on the desk.

'Come here,' she said, gesturing for Genetta to assume the same position that she had taken before.

And Genetta did. She knelt, eager to feel Marie quaking as she drove her over the edge. Greedily, she put her thumbs on either side of Marie's sex and split her wide. She looked at the pink meat there, the way the inner lips wanted to cling together, but the fat outer ones yielded to her grasp. Marie's hair was trimmed neatly into a black, silky little triangle. Experimenting, Genetta pressed her nose into that dark nest, smelling Marie's saltiness, then stretched her tongue down to touch the right spot.

'That feels so good,' Marie whispered. 'But I want a lot more from you.'

With that, she held the back of Genetta's head and pulled her face even closer. Genetta opened her mouth wider and darted her tongue deeper, and Marie seemed to love it. She entwined her fingers in Genetta's hair and bore down on her face. Genetta reached up and pushed two fingers into Marie, next to her delving tongue. Marie groaned and her legs fell open even wider on either side of Genetta's head.

With her feet in the air, Marie fumbled to open the compact. 'I want to see my snatch,' she said with a crudity that conflicted with her usual image of composed femininity, pushing Genetta back a little.

Genetta helped her boss, and guided Marie's hand until they had the mirror right in front of her sex.

'Oh God,' Marie whispered when she saw her glistening labia and round, swollen bud. 'Make that your meal, my dear.' She dropped the compact on the floor, and then arched her back, pushing her mound down and out. 'Make me come now,' she gasped, as Genetta swirled her fingers inside, feeling the tight muscles of Marie's pussy contract.

Attentive to her boss's wishes, Genetta concentrated her ministrations back on Marie's clit. First she nibbled at the entire fleshy structure, ignoring the erect bud that clamoured for her specific mindfulness. Then, growing bold with her tongue, she pushed its fleshiness against the underside of Marie's nub. Taking a long lick, she pointed the tip and began to return the treatment that Marie had given her.

Marie's reaction was almost animalistic. Her growls filled the small space of the office as Genetta poked, caressed and flicked her centre. She hummed for a moment, and then growled again. Then, clamping Genetta's head tightly between her hands and thighs, she pushed her heels into Genetta's back and came with a gasping, shuddering whimper.

'Oh, save me,' Marie sighed afterwards. She stretched her arms above her head, obviously luxuriating in the feelings that Genetta had given her. Then she said, quite clearly, 'Now get away from me.'

Somewhat taken aback and upset, Genetta moved too quickly and fell back on her bottom, her head hitting the desk.

Marie stared and shook her head. 'You need some decorum – some training,' she said cruelly and dismissively. 'I think I'll claim you for a little while, Genetta. It will do you a great deal of good. And your first lessons will teach you how to be my little puppy.'

Chapter Three

The collar fitted comfortably enough. Marie pushed two fingers between the black leather and Genetta's throat, exactly as a careful owner ensures her dog's physical welfare before putting on the leash.

Genetta closed her eyes and raised her chin, knowing that Marie would caress her jaw for a moment – and certainly, that's what happened. The mistress's fingertips lingered on the slave's skin, and Genetta felt the thrill of voluptuous longing simmer through her.

'You're going to be a smash hit tonight,' Marie told her. 'So many people are so looking forward to seeing my new work of art.'

'Your creation?'

'More than that – my puppy; my darling, well-behaved, trained puppy girl. Tell me, my dear, are you looking forward to having company over tonight?'

'I think so,' Genetta answered honestly.

Marie stared at her for a long moment, and Genetta maintained her own gaze at Marie's mouth. That was as close to looking in her owner's eyes as she was allowed to get. She watched as Marie's lips parted, and then sneered before she spoke.

'And when are you going to ask the next appropriate question?' she asked.

At first Genetta could only answer by frowning. She was perplexed by Marie's question, never mind thinking of another one herself, and then she flinched a little as

Marie positively snarled at her.

'You are supposed to ask if there's anything you can do to prepare the house or yourself or me for their arrival!' she spat.

Genetta recoiled from the anger in Marie's voice. 'Sorry, ma'am,' she apologised.

'Genny, Genny, whatever am I going to do with you?' Marie touched her jaw again, but the gesture was not as soft as it had been the first time.

'Train me, ma'am,' the slave answered. 'Please, train me how to please you.'

'You can please me by learning when and how to take the initiative in certain areas. Sexually, I will always dominate you, but when it comes to the small things – ironing clothes, picking up around the house, giving me manicures – you need to learn when to step forward.'

'But, ma'am, you don't always like my suggestions,' Genetta protested. 'Last week I asked if you wanted me to brush your hair, and you hated that idea.'

'Just because I reject certain things that you bring up at certain times, doesn't mean you should stop coming forward with your thoughts.'

'What if there are things that I want to do?' Genetta asked. 'Should I just go ahead and do them?'

'What kind of question is that, Genetta?' Marie snapped, and Genetta could hear Marie's voice getting that icy edge.

'Well, if there's something special I want to do for you, should I go ahead and do it? Make a certain dinner, for example, or something like that?'

'No, you must always ask my permission,' Marie answered after a pause. 'You must always ask.'

'In every instance?'

'Yes, in every instance.' Her answer came quickly that

time, as if she had completely made up her mind on the issue.

But Genetta felt compelled to press it. 'So no surprises, then?'

'What did I just say to you?' Marie said impatiently. 'No, no surprises, none whatsoever. Do you need a spanking to make the rule sink in?'

'No, that's not necessary,' Genetta answered. 'I understand completely. You don't want to find out that I've done something after I've done it. I must come to you and ask if I am permitted to act on an idea I have, and only after receiving your answer may I continue.'

'And not just having received an answer, Genetta,' Marie clarified sternly. 'I must say yes. Do you understand that? If I tell you that you can't do something, then you can't do it. Your asking isn't going to mean that I always grant permission.'

'That's a bit harsh, isn't it? Where do my desires fit in?' But as soon as Genetta had blurted the remarks, she wished she could bite them back.

Marie's lips went pencil-line thin, as if she, too, wanted to bite something. 'Your desires are well below mine, slave,' she hissed. 'Your desires should be to please me, and gaining my permission before you act is the most important thing you can do. So coming up with ideas that you know will gain my permission and that please me in and of themselves are your only desires.'

Genetta purposefully put a blank expression on her face. She wasn't convinced and needed to hide the fact – so changing the subject was apropos right now.

'What can I do to ready the house or you, mistress?' she asked sweetly.

Marie smiled a ghost of a smile. 'Very good, that you

eventually got there,' she said unconvincingly. 'Actually, the preparation I want has to do with you. Put on the red dress, the short one; the one with the skirt that sashays nicely as you walk and turn. And wear no panties.'

'That dress will look particularly good with my black collar,' Genetta observed.

'Yes, it will,' Marie said a little abruptly. 'Why else do you think I suggested it?

'Red heels, as well,' she went on. 'No stockings on this occasion, and it goes without saying that you're not to wear tights.'

'Yes, ma'am, that does go without saying,' Genetta concurred. 'I'll go and get ready right now.'

'I suspect that our first guests will arrive within the next ten minutes,' Marie informed her slave, 'so hurry yourself up. I want to put the leash on you before they show.'

When Genetta returned, wearing nothing but the short dress and the heels – just as she had been instructed – Marie held up a rhinestone-studded, black leather leash. It was precisely the kind that certain people used to walk their spoiled pet Chihuahuas.

'The collar is to show how devoted you are to me,' Marie informed Genetta, 'whilst the daintiness of the leash is to show how light my touch is and needs to be in controlling that devotion.'

She snapped the leash onto the collar. Then she stepped back, holding the end of the thin strap, and surveyed Genetta's appearance. 'Quite lovely,' she murmured, and then wrapping the leash around her hand, she drew her slave closer.

When Genetta was within her reach, Marie slipped her hand up under the short skirt of the red dress. The slave gasped as Marie's fingertips brushed the delicate ruff of hair covering her mound, and closed her eyes rapturously as her mistress slipped her finger into the moistness there.

Marie withdrew her hand and raised it to her own mouth. With the very tip of her tongue she licked her finger. Genetta watched and wriggled to show her mistress how she yearned to feel her tongue probe her wet sex.

Marie entered Genetta's slipperiness again. This time she pushed the back of her hand against the slave's hungry pussy, slid against Genetta's ready cleft, and ended by grinding a knuckle against her swollen clit.

Genetta rode down on the pressure. 'Horny bitch,' Marie said with satisfaction, laughing softly. 'You're ready for it at any time, aren't you?'

The horny, wet, eager slave reached down and took Marie's wrist. Holding her mistress's hand firmly against herself, she began masturbating faster and harder.

Footsteps sounded in the hallway, and at the noise Genetta panicked a little and let go of Marie's arm, but the mistress kept pressing against her little whore's slick pussy. 'Let everyone see what a randy little slut you truly are,' she whispered. 'Let them see how you get yourself off any way you can.'

Blushing with shame, but unable to deny her mistress, Genetta shuffled her feet a little wider apart and with a conscious effort, rode the hand that lingered tight up between her thighs. She shut her eyes and ears to the presence of anyone else. Her mind was centred intently on her pleasure and what she needed.

She did hear, though, the throaty mocking sound of Marie's laughter. 'She's very good, isn't she?' Genetta heard her mistress say, and those words, praising her, made the slave cascade into a wonderful knee-trembling, leg-shivering orgasm.

Someone was behind her, reaching around her, holding her up in their arms. 'Excellent powers of concentration,' Marie said, and Genetta heard appreciative laughter as the throbbing between her legs grew less along with the delicious spasms.

When Marie tugged on the leash Genetta opened her eyes, blinked, and looked around. A crowd of about a dozen people had gathered in the lounge where she stood with her owner, and everyone was watching her closely. Several of the women licked their lips, as if they could already taste her, and the men had looks of utter lust on their faces.

Living with Marie, working with Marie and the girls at the office, being completely in Marie's thrall, Genetta hadn't had contact with men in weeks. She sensed that Marie liked it that way, too – and Genetta thought that Marie did not want the threat of her having any sexual desires or needs that another woman could not fully satisfy.

Sexual desires and needs... Genetta's mind moved catlike among her inventory of favourite positions. Her eyes slithered down the torso, hips and legs of the man nearest her, and after admiring how he was put together, she calculated how much he would like it if she straddled him and went for a frenzied ride.

His partner moved up and took her place beside him, giving Genetta a cool look. Genetta returned a puzzled one, as if to say, 'I thought we were all here for fun and sharing,' but never mind. There were plenty more men besides that one.

And the man's woman wasn't the only person who noticed Genetta's wandering eyes. Marie gave her a sharp tug from behind, and the thick collar yanked against Genetta's throat. It embarrassed her when her breath caught with a sharp gasp, and she did not much care for the way the woman's challenging glare turned to one of condescending smugness.

Genetta looked the man in question squarely in the eye for the first time, and she promised him, silently, that she would give him everything he wanted as soon as they could get their bodies together. The risk she took in giving him that kind of sultry look did not cost her anything; at least not immediately, for Marie had not noticed. The other woman had, but Genetta cared little about her reaction now. She was more interested in teaching that priggish cow a lesson.

After holding the man's gaze for a long moment, Genetta turned to see what Marie was doing, and saw her owner was distracted by some pretty girls who stood at the back of the room, away from everyone else.

Marie held the leash at arm's length, and her other hand gesticulated as she spoke to the girls. Slowly, Genetta moved closer to Marie's side and waited for her chance to join the conversation.

It would not take long. Marie was holding forth on the subject of owning and training delightful girls whose bodies needed more sustained pleasure than a mere man could give.

'Really, my dear, men are out for their own satisfaction,' she was saying. 'It's rare to find a single one who's willing to stop dribbling from his cock and start rubbing with his tongue. Or fingers, in the worst case.'

'How can you be so sure?' asked one of the girls. 'Given your preferences for—'

'Oh, darling, I'm not a naïve dyke,' Marie interrupted,

laughing haughtily. 'I've been with plenty of men, believe me. What do you think drove me to women?'

The gaggle of young things giggled, and Genetta saw that some of them were quite nervous at listening to Marie's forward invitation to experience the velvet tongue of another woman. And when she looked at Marie, she could see that her mistress very much enjoyed the seduction of virgins to Sappho's ways.

Marie caught Genetta watching her and winding the leash around her forearm, pulled the slave close. Her eyes half shut with desire, she glanced sideways at the gorgeous girls. She purred into Genetta's ear and said, in a smoky voice, 'I bet they get so wet…' Her voice trailed off and Genetta could see that Marie's mind was taking her on a journey between young, white thighs.

'Do you want to play with anyone in particular?' Genetta asked; all of these people around, all of them potential partners, were making her incredibly hot.

'Mmm, that's a very tasty idea,' Marie answered. She put her hand on Genetta's waist, slid her palm up her side, and did not stop until she was cupping a firm breast. She thumbed Genetta's nipple as she looked thoughtfully at the watching girls. 'They're first-timers to this kind of thing – almost certainly feeling somewhat out of their depth.'

'How did they learn about our party?' Genetta asked. Her breath was growing ragged with excitement.

'Oh, friends of friends,' Marie explained. 'Some other girls I know thought that these little things would enjoy some fun. And as the evening goes on…' Marie turned to look behind them at the cliques drinking wine, taking hors d'oeuvres and talking, '…I trust there will be enough activities and opportunities for everyone; regardless of expertise, or innocence.'

With her last words, she turned back to gaze hungrily at the new girls. All the while she kept a little tension on Genetta's leash and steady, circular pressure going around her nipple.

It was Genetta's turn to purr, and she did so, moaning low in her throat as a question formed in her mind. 'M-mistress...' she ventured carefully, 'you like to... to recruit, don't you?'

Her words made Marie focus on her and draw close. Mistress's mouth was very close to slave's, and Genetta felt Marie's lips move as she answered.

'Yes, I like to teach about pleasure,' she agreed. 'And train to get respect.'

'You've taught me so much about my body and how to use it – how to really feel everything that happens to me,' Genetta said, and her soft lips moved against Marie's as she spoke.

'And I have so much more to show you, my darling.'

Their kiss finally happened. Genetta opened her mouth to the sensuous softness of Marie's probing tongue. Her lips caught the fullness of her mistress's exploration and Genetta's knees, already weak from coming so exquisitely only a few minutes before, trembled again.

Marie pulled her mouth away, and left Genetta's lips parted and wet like a blossom in dew. 'Isn't she a delightful wench?' Marie asked the onlookers, and murmurs of ascent rose and fell. 'I was going to have her perform some of her lovely puppy tricks for you all, but she seems to offer more pleasure on two legs.'

At that, one of the delectable girls stepped forward. 'May I kiss her too?' she asked.

Genetta opened her heavy-lidded eyes to read Marie's

expression. She'd had the definite feeling over the past few weeks she'd spent under Marie's tutelage that while the mistress could indulge herself in the odd dalliance, any extracurricular pleasures for Genetta were out of the question.

That's why Marie's amused smile surprised her – and the reply shocked her even more.

'Yes, you may kiss her, my darling – but perhaps a little later,' Marie said. 'First, though, I want you to try your hand at something more daring – more in line with tonight's theme. I want you to redden her delicious bottom for us.'

The girl laughed uncertainly. 'Um, I really don't think that's my style,' she said.

'But how can you know what you're inclined to like until you try everything on offer?' Marie reasoned. 'I'm willing to permit you to dominate my personal slave. I've spent a great deal of precious time training her to be attuned to all of my wishes and my deepest desires, and you will be insulting my hospitality if you refuse my extremely generous offer.'

Genetta met the girl's dark brown doe eyes. The girl looked a little confused by Marie's explanation.

'Just say yes,' Genetta softly prompted. 'What's your name?'

'Claudia,' the girl answered.

'Just say yes, Claudia,' Genetta prompted again. 'Let my mistress give me to you for your use and pleasure.'

Marie gave Genetta a stern, warning look.

'For a little while,' Genetta said quickly, smiling at Marie in an effort to disarm her mistress's flashing jealousy.

Claudia looked from mistress to slave. Genetta could tell by the look on the girl's face – the tight smile and downcast eyes – and her distracted way of pulling down her skirt that she felt trapped somehow by the negotiations taking place around her. If she were not made to feel more in control of the situation, there was no way she would be able to learn her first lesson in being a competent dominant.

'Would you like to include one of your friends in a session?' Genetta asked, searching for the situation that would make Claudia happier and more at ease with what was developing.

'Genetta,' Marie snapped. 'Remember our discussion earlier. Remember what I told you, and what I expect.'

'Yes, mistress,' Genetta answered quickly. 'Would it please you if I figured out a way to help Claudia feel comfortable in joining us?' she asked, knowing instantly to what Marie was referring.

Marie narrowed her eyes a little before she answered. 'Yes,' she said slowly, in a way that communicated her measured consideration of Genetta's request. 'Yes, it would please me. Go ahead and sort something out with her. You have my permission.'

Genetta nodded and smiled at Marie to show her own happiness and gratitude at having her question answered quickly and positively. 'Come on then, Claudia,' she said, turning her attention back to their could-be playmate. 'Do you want to invite some company along?'

'And how many girls, exactly, are you thinking about entertaining?' Marie broke in.

Genetta assessed the curvaceous bodies standing together nearby. 'As many as I can handle,' she said, and licked her lips.

'My darling slave, remember, I didn't agree for Claudia to kiss you. On your upper or your lower lips. And I certainly did not agree to sexual contact of any other sort. I told Claudia that she could play at being your dom this evening. Now tell me, my sweet – how many of those playful doms do you think you can take on?'

Genetta flexed her shoulders back, then forward and rolled them provocatively at the end of her stretch. 'I can obey however many new doms it would take to give you satisfaction, mistress.'

'A perfect answer, Genetta,' Marie said, with evident satisfaction. 'Now tell me, do you want Claudia?'

Genetta lingered over Claudia's big dark eyes, her white throat, the delicate tinge of blue veins that showed through the fair skin of her chest, her full round breasts that swayed ever so gently under the tight silk of her blouse, her full hips undulating within her close-fitting skirt.

'Yes, mistress, I want her,' Genetta confirmed excitedly.

'Then you shall not have her,' Marie teased. 'I think I'll take Claudia for myself tonight, as I rather like her demure ways. You, Genetta my dear, fall prey to those chop-licking whores among Claudia's friends. I've been watching them and I'm sure some know what to do with a good slave's body. Just as surely as I've got plans for Claudia's.'

With that, Marie dropped the leash and extended her hand to the new girl. Without question Claudia took Marie's fingers in her own and the two made their way back through the crowd that had been amassing in the house since the negotiations had begun.

Genetta watched her mistress's back as she disappeared with their new acquaintance. One moment ago all of this had seemed a delightful game, bound to take Genetta on a foray into new, delicious experiences. But that had been when she felt some control over events. Then with a wrenching twist Marie asserted her own authority again, claimed the night's prize, and left Genetta to play the submissive lipstick lesbian to these new girls.

And she did not like it.

Turning to face the group, who were still hanging in the shadowy edges of light at the room's far end, Genetta smiled. Her pride was hurt, she was jealous for Marie's attentions and she had wanted to bury her face in Claudia, but no one else could know or understand the three-pronged attack her ego had just suffered.

She wrapped the leash around her forearm, arranging it to look serpentine. Looking back at the girls, who were all staring at her, she took a few steps towards them.

'The cat's away, my lovelies,' she said. 'So shall we play?'

She looked over their beautiful young faces and marvelled at the infinite gorgeous ways that women were created. All shared a pouting lower lip, large round eyes and fragile-looking jaws. All were ultra-feminine.

None had Claudia's manner of being demure but forward, though. Quality like that was hard to find, and Genetta knew that was why Marie had snapped up their new treasure. She wanted to take that girl to bed and explore her many psychic folds and bodily curves.

A saucy looking redheaded girl broke the staring contest between the group and Genetta. Her glossy red lips, biteable as a candy apple, pursed and pouted before she spoke. Finally, looking at Genetta with aquamarine eyes darting, she said, 'Marie has left you in our control then, has she?'

Genetta smiled indulgently. She had been in this lifestyle for just a little while, but she was obviously more initiated to its nuances than were this inexperienced group. 'Not really,' she said. 'Marie's my mistress, so only she can top me.'

'But if you're a real bottom, you should be able to serve and please anyone,' the redhead rejoined.

Genetta admired the girl's dewy make-up before she took a deep breath and explained. 'I'm not a "bottom". I don't get off on having things done to me by whomever. I'm a submissive – I like to serve—'

'Right,' the spunky little thing interrupted. 'I know your gaff. You like to serve your owner. You said, though, that you could handle any number of girls tonight. Were you lying to your mistress when you claimed that? Or will you stand by what you told her?'

'What's your name?' Genetta asked.

'Rory.'

'Rory...' Genetta mused. 'It suits you, with your gorgeous mane of red hair. But I wonder something.'

'And what would that be?'

'I wonder if you could argue so well with my delicious pussy spread over your mouth.'

Rory stifled a giggle. 'Actually, I was wondering the same thing about you,' she said. 'I was imagining how you'd look with your nose riding my bush.'

'Oh, you're not shaven?' Genetta asked.

Rory shook her head, her sparkling eyes never leaving Genetta. 'No, I'm not,' she disclosed freely. 'Are you?'

'No,' Genetta admitted.

'So why don't you and me follow Marie and Claudia,' Rory suggested mischievously.

Genetta looked deep into her sparkling eyes. 'You're not really new to any of this, are you?'

Rory shrugged, her narrow shoulders rising and falling under the spaghetti straps of her shimmering blue dress.

'I'm not new to imagining things I'd love to do between another girl's legs, no,' she said bluntly.

'And I'm not new to figuring out ways to discipline naughty girls, either,' a new voice said from behind Genetta, and as she turned to see who had spoken, Rory snatched the handle of the leash from her hand and yanked it tight. Genetta caught her breath as it bit into her arm, and she just managed to catch a glimpse of the woman she'd been taunting earlier by staring at her male partner.

The woman clasped Genetta's other wrist as she walked around to join Rory.

'Kate, hello,' Rory said. She looked from Genetta to Kate, then back again like a lioness watching the flick of its prey's tail.

'Let's take her,' Kate said, without so much as a nod in greeting to Rory. Rory did not seem to mind, though; she turned back towards the group of girls and a few of them stepped forward.

With slow, slinky movements they came up and surrounded Rory. Genetta realised that the entire pride of she-lions were about to take her into their lair – and their control.

Meeting their eyes – brown, blue, hazel, green – one piercing stare after the next, she unwound her forearm from the lead that Rory held tight. When she was done, Rory smoothed it, taking the kinks out and running its length between thumb and forefinger.

Genetta watched her hand move so expertly over the piece of thin leather, then raised her eyes. Rory was staring straight at her with an intensity that built by the second.

'Ready, darling?' Rory's lips moved to form the words, but they delayed reaching Genetta's ears. It was as if something had slowed her mind, dampened her hearing.

Yet her eyes and skin took in every stimulus. Every one of their breaths touched her flesh like the touch of snakes' forked tongues.

But she nodded.

Rory passed the looped handle of the leash over to Kate. Genetta watched it change hands. Rory's nimble fingers brushed against Kate's outstretched, white palm. The latter closed her fingers around it and Genetta saw her long nails, painted a deep, dark purple. They looked as if they'd already been dipped in the blood dripping from the jugular of one sacrificial victim tonight.

Intrigued and a little scared by what Kate might have in mind, Genetta followed when her temporary owner tugged at the collar around her neck.

They walked out of the lounge and into the dining room. The mahogany table stood on its clawed feet in the centre of the space. The chairs, though, were pulled away from their usual places and lined up with their backs against the walls.

Sitting on the chairs was a variety of instruments designed for exquisite torture. The first one Genetta spied had a variety of floggers on it, the second one specialised in martinets only. Riding crops were propped against the back of the third and lashes dangled from the seat of the fourth. The burden of the fifth was simple: paddles, including wooden spoons and spatulas. The sixth was unused.

Genetta's attention was so riveted by the display, she hardly noticed that the troupe of young women had slinked quietly into the room behind her. They spread out, taking up stations next to chairs, as if preordained.

Kate jerked the lead and Genetta followed her closer to the table. Glancing down at it and nodding brusquely, Kate gave a silent instruction – Genetta was to bend over.

So she did so, very slowly. Ever so carefully, she parted her high-heeled shoes on the floor and bent forward. Marie would be extremely annoyed if she left palm prints on the shining reddish surface, so she tipped her upper body, jutted out her bottom, and tensed her stomach muscles to hold herself up.

'You thought you might enjoy my man tonight, but no,' Kate accused, hissing in her ear. She pulled the lead to the other side as she crossed behind Genetta, and then leaned in to taunt her some more. 'But rest assured, we're going to enjoy you, very, very much.'

She stepped away, and still gripping the lead, she strutted to the side of the table. Genetta shifted just enough to prevent Kate pulling her over.

'Ladies,' Kate began, 'tonight we have a lesson in store. It is meant to allow each and every one of you to acquire new knowledge and abilities. It is also going to show cheeky, whorish submissives a thing or two about getting up to trouble with another mistress's toy.'

Genetta closed her eyes and cursed her own flirtatious, man-hungry ways. Then opening her eyes again, she watched Kate warily.

'In fact,' the woman continued, 'tonight this slave will suffer the humiliation of being beaten by another slave, at my behest and according to my instructions.'

Of course, Genetta thought, she should not have assumed; just because Kate was fairly petite did not mean she could not rule over her more imposing male partner.

'Daniel!' Kate called.

And the short hairstyle Kate wore was another clue, Genetta thought; nothing for a man to grab and use as reins.

She heard heavier footsteps fall on the wood floor. That must be him, she decided, but did not dare turn to look; Kate was clearly spiteful enough without added provocation.

He took a place just behind Genetta, a little to her left. She could sense him there; she could feel the ripples travelling towards her through the air from his slight movements.

She did see Kate turn and give him a smile, but those dark eyes, shadowed by the dim light, looked cold.

'So, my young ladies,' Kate said, 'tonight we will choose an implement from this gorgeous and inviting array. Daniel will demonstrate its proper application on Genetta's bottom, and then those of you who would like to try your hand will be given a chance to do so.'

Kate dropped the lead then and took her rightful place at the head of the table. Sitting in the one empty chair and settling herself by stretching out one leg, catlike, she gave an order. 'Begin giving Daniel the toys.'

Someone passed a flogger first, but other than the sound of stiletto spikes tapping against the floor as the girl took a step forward to pass it, and then back to her station, the room was silent. Genetta looked around at the faces, evenly spaced against the russet red wall. When her eye caught Rory's, the sassy redhead minx gave her a two-fingered salute with a difference: she put her hand to her mouth and flicked her pink tongue out through the middle of the V.

Genetta's reflexes kicked in suddenly when Daniel trailed the flogger's suede tresses along her back. She rolled her shoulders at the tickle, at once trying to dislodge it, but feel even more.

In a slow, teasing figure eight, Daniel continued to trace

the flogger over her back. ‘Faster,’ Kate snapped, and he began to pick up the speed. As he moved the weapon more quickly he began to pull it farther away from Genetta’s back. It started to land on her skin with slapping sounds. Every loose leather tip stung her just a little, but at the same time, warmed her. Genetta could feel the blood rushing to the surface of her insulted back.

The girls around the room were crowding in. They were drawn to the beating, getting closer as Daniel’s swings got higher and the flogger cut down harder.

Genetta glanced wildly around as her torturer’s breathing increased behind her. He was reaching towards a full extension of his swinging arm, bringing the heavy flogger down with each stroke. The separate straps, just moments before so gentle, were now travelling at full speed and sweeping down onto her as one blow. Daniel rained the flogger’s punishment down on her bare back, and Genetta arched her spine, futilely trying to escape.

‘Enough,’ Kate said loudly, and immediately the flogger began kissing Genetta’s burnt flesh. Daniel slackened the pace and the force until once again the flogger’s fingers caressed her shoulder blades.

‘And who’s next to have a go at tanning this slave’s hide?’ Kate asked. ‘Who wants to dominate such a beaten wench?’

‘I do,’ a voice from behind Genetta said, and she could not have turned to see who it was even if she had wanted to – her skin felt as if it were on the verge of charred, like Rory the redhead might feel if she’d been on a Mediterranean beach for too long after a dark British winter.

The telling noise of high-heeled shoes on the hard floor told Genetta that her new tormentor was drawing near.

‘And what would you like to use, my darling?’

Genetta started. That was Marie's voice. And the other, to whom she spoke, must be Claudia.

A different kind of heat began to sear Genetta's face. She felt humiliated, the lowest of any submissive. Marie had just permitted the new girl to pleasure her – or, for all Genetta knew, Marie had done the pleasuring – and now she was permitting this interloper to abuse *her*. To abuse Genetta – Marie's personal servant and slave!

'A crop,' Claudia replied.

'You want to treat my puppy to some pony type training?' Marie asked.

'Yes, ma'am, if it pleases you.'

Genetta nearly felt sick. Claudia had watched some videos, that's all her courtesy meant. She had learnt the protocol of titles. That did not mean that she could bend her own will to serve Marie's darkest needs, not the way Genetta could.

The thoughts cascaded through her mind, jealous dominos, clicking angrily as they fell. And at the same time she watched manicured hands deliver the crop to the girl who had Marie's attention for at least the night.

Genetta turned her gaze to Kate. You've won, she communicated as best she could. She could understand the woman's jealousy now.

Kate stared back at her, dark eyes swallowing Genetta's silent humiliation, submission, and apology. Her crimson lips parted in a smile – but froze before the approving look was complete.

Genetta resigned herself to a thrashing.

Claudia popped the crop, probably against her own thigh.

'My, but you handle that well!' Marie exclaimed.

Genetta bowed her head and Kate said, 'Any time you are ready, Claudia, her bottom is yours.'

They need never know Genetta was done in by all this, she decided, and eased her bottom back and out as the first blow fell.

Claudia hit her with the full length of the crop, completely across her buttocks, hip to hip. Over and over. At first Genetta concentrated on the slapping sound that the leather loop at the crop's tip made upon every connection.

But the pain soon won.

It obliterated her. The stinging, then the burning, then the knowledge that she was being marked; closing her eyes and imagining the stipples rise on her fair skin. It was all too much.

And then it was over. Genetta opened her tear-filled eyes and let the drops fall onto the shining wood below. They beaded separately, then joined and shimmered.

Her senses were newly awakened by the acute pain her bottom was suffering, the barely dulled ache in every inch of flesh stretched across her upper back.

A shadow moved up beside her. Genetta bent her head, inclining her ear towards the breathing.

'Now you've met Kate,' Marie whispered. 'And your training – the lessons you so sorely need from me to make you behave – has only just begun.'

Chapter Four

'Filthy little bitch – look at you beg for it.'

Marie tugged the dog lead, the other end of which was attached to Genetta's collar. In response, she rose out of her puppy dog stretch and stopped wiggling her bottom in the air. She wanted to show Marie the silent servitude that she had learnt in the past two weeks since her abject humiliation at the party.

'This chain connects us. Top and bottom.' She gave it another sharp pull and Genetta lurched forward a little from the tug on the back of her neck, but still did not move: her mistress had not told her to.

Marie squatted down in front of her, and Genetta stared longingly at how her trousers stretched tight over her thighs. She did not dare raise her eyes to meet Marie's or to glance at her face, but she was free to gaze over that body with a sex-starved, needy look.

Marie slid her index finger between the padding of Genetta's wide leather collar and her throat. Genetta tilted her head so that Marie's knuckles rubbed across her jawbone as she withdrew her hand. Then she lifted her eyes to stare at Marie's navel as she rose before her, and saw Marie lift her arm. She must have looked down at her watch.

'I fancy some lunch,' she announced. 'Don't you, little doggy?'

Genetta crawled forward one tentative step and rubbed her cheek against the side of Marie's knee in answer.

'Little doggies have to have food and drink,' Marie went on. 'Especially little bitches in heat who can't get enough.'

Genetta let her head drop a little at the name-calling, but Marie dragged sideways at the leash, and Genetta followed the indication to move to the left.

When she was perfectly in place, ready to come to heel when Marie walked, her mistress reached down and pushed her fingers between Genetta's bottom cheeks. The tip of Marie's finger circled her anus, and Genetta felt herself squeeze and contract involuntarily. She cringed, because she knew what would happen now.

And Marie didn't disappoint. She gave Genetta a smart smack on the bottom for her impertinent movement, and then resumed the finger rimming. Genetta willed herself to be still for her mistress.

'Mmm,' Marie growled, 'getting into this would be very nice. Little bitch dogs love it from behind. They take it up the arse, they take it up the pussy, they take it any way they can get it.' She paused. 'Am I right?'

Genetta whimpered and lowered her breasts to the floor, opening and exposing her buttocks for her dom. Marie slid her fingers down into Genetta's waiting pussy and slipped them back and forth... slowly, slowly.

'Only a very nasty girl gets this wet from being treated like an animal,' Marie sneered. Genetta arched her back and pushed her bottom up for Marie's convenience. 'What a well trained puppy you are,' the owner said softly.

She pulled her hand away, and Genetta closed her eyes to hide her chagrin. All day Marie had exercised an enormous amount of control over her slave – and herself. It was easy enough for Genetta to obey and be naked and crawl around after her, even on the hardwood floors. But how Marie kept herself from demanding passionate oral service confused Genetta.

'Undo me,' Marie ordered.

Genetta lifted her face, but kept her eyes cast down. 'Undo your zip, ma'am?'

'That's what I said.' She smacked Genetta lazily across the face. 'Pay more attention to me.'

Tears rose to Genetta's eyes from even that small tap. She knew that Marie knew how much she hated having her face hit or threatened in any way – that's precisely why Marie was so indolent when she did it. Marie was showing Genetta that she could do it at her leisure, without any real anger behind it. Yet by pretending to strip the punishment of any meaning, Marie succeeded in loading it with a deep, degrading, perfect reminder to Genetta of her humiliation before her mistress.

Genetta dragged her fingertips across Marie's crotch, still on the outside of her trousers. Slowly, she moved up to the zip and pulled it down.

'Ma'am, please.' She intoned the words under her breath, begging Marie quietly to release both of them from the puppy training long enough to rub against each other, to fuck their bodies together, and to come.

'Pull them off.'

Genetta gently grasped the waistband of Marie's trousers, along with the elastic band of her panties. With a tug and a long pull, she dragged everything down.

Marie's sex pushed forward into her face. Slyly, Genetta gave her clit a few butterfly licks before she held the trousers and panties tight to the floor. Marie stepped out of the clothes and stood in her bare feet, clothed only in a tight, long-sleeved, jewel-necked, black shirt.

Genetta looked up at Marie's full breasts, but no further. She never risked a look into Marie's eyes during her puppy dog training. Marie had made it clear with admonitions and slaps that Genetta was not to – not even with the most supplicant of glances. But she could tell that Marie was staring down at her right now, relishing the sight as she demurely awaited further orders.

Marie sighed a low, luscious sound. 'Go to the bureau and retrieve our friends,' she said in her dark, smoky voice.

Genetta crawled to the piece of furniture and opened the heavy bottom drawer. Several black boxes and leather bags were lying in it. She pulled out one box, covered in a faux snakeskin with rhinestones on the top. It was gaudy, but Genetta had learnt that underneath Marie's cool, ultra-professional exterior, her tastes in sex were very nearly meretricious. She wanted everything to be filthy, grungy, vulgar and wet.

Opening the silver latches, Genetta felt her pussy moisten even more with excitement. This was one of her favourite parts of the day – when Marie finally possessed her completely.

She took out the large dildo and laid it on the floor in front of her knees, then carefully put the box away. Next, she retrieved a little leather drawstring bag. Opening it, she emptied its contents onto the floor, on top of the dildo.

Genetta knew this was Marie's favourite part of the day too, because Genetta put the vibrating plastic scorpion over her snatch for her, its pointed tail pressing up into her bottom.

She placed the leather bag back into the drawer and pushed it shut, then put the black leather harness of the dildo and the elastic of the scorpion between her teeth and dragged both items over to her mistress. Marie bent and took them from Genetta's mouth, and Genetta, resting back on her haunches, watched Marie's hips as she donned the toys.

Marie stepped into the white elastic first, arranging the scorpion over her dark-haired pussy. Genetta didn't want to presume or anticipate, so she waited patiently until her mistress said, 'Sort it now, puppy.'

Hastily, Genetta rose to her knees and touched the ribbed back of the vibrator. She ran her fingers over it, moving the scorpion's sting towards Marie's anus.

When the point of the tail was at the right spot, with her middle finger, Genetta pressed on it. Her fingertip found Marie's tight entrance and she slowly guided the scorpion's tail inside.

It slipped in easily, and Genetta gave it a gentle push to ensure it was lodged enough to give her mistress pleasure when she turned the machine on. Then she backed away, head lowered – she was glad to perform her service to Marie's pleasure, and she made sure that her posture showed it. She raised her eyes only to watch Marie finish dressing.

The dildo's harness slipped up over the woman's creamy thighs, and her nimble fingers fastened it quickly and tightly. The large, long, flesh-coloured penis stuck straight out, bobbing threateningly.

'Worship it,' Marie ordered softly, and Genetta rocked forward onto her hands and crawled closer. 'Treat me like you would a man,' her mistress ordered.

The slave puppy did not pause. She took the latex cock in her fist and stroked it a few times, then took it in her fingertips and pretended to jerk it off quickly, and as she was attending to the cock's needs, Marie turned on a switch and the scorpion purred to life. Marie growled low in her throat, and Genetta could feel the vibrations through the cock in her hand.

'Now, deep throat me,' the woman directed.

Genetta opened her jaw wide and slid her lips over the dildo's girth and length. She sucked it deep into her throat, holding her lips tight around it, then slid back out to its helmet. Then she pushed her tongue out over her lower teeth and took it to the back of her throat again.

The dildo was bigger than any cock she had ever sucked, and it required great self-control for her to be able to take it like this. Marie sometimes wanted to gag her with it, and would put her hands on the back of Genetta's head to pull her face into her crotch.

None of that happened this time, though. Marie let her get the artificial penis good and wet with her mouth, then moved behind her and knelt on the floor, between her legs. She grabbed her hips roughly and centred them in front of her. Genetta strained backwards, rocking into Marie, trying desperately to feel woman flesh against woman flesh.

Marie plunged into her with might. Genetta gasped and pushed against the floor with the heels of her hands, holding herself steady for the onslaught of pumps and thrusts that Marie ground into her.

'Oh, Genetta,' the dominatrix grunted, and the slave thrilled to hear her mistress use her name.

The driving cock ceased as suddenly as it had started. 'Genetta,' Marie whispered as she began to slide in and out of her slowly. She pushed in, held the cock deep inside her for a moment, and then pulled back.

Genetta smiled to feel Marie, to really feel her screwing that hole. And she knew that the scorpion, its body vibrating over Marie's clit, its tail digging into her bottom, was pleasuring her mistress, too. But the dildo was the centre of Genetta and her world right now. She could live forever in this moment, with Marie inside her, treating her like a whore and a plaything.

'This is how you know I care about my puppy,' Marie said in her low voice as her fake staff continued rubbing in and out of Genetta's very real, very wet pussy. 'You please me very much, so I give you the only thing that can please you. This cock; I give it to you.'

Genetta moaned her thanks as Marie kept moving in and out of her methodically. They melted into the slow groove of their screwing. Marie began grunting with every inward thrust, and Genetta groaned to feel how the cock's thickness opened her passage and rubbed her insides.

Marie entered so slowly, penetrating her inch by inch. She did not ride hard, so this was not the animal encounter Genetta had been wanting since she woke up at the foot of Marie's bed that morning, naked but for the dog collar. This was deliberate, careful work. This was Marie showing her that she had mastered herself long before she had mastered Genetta.

Marie cursed before she addressed Genetta again. 'You're such a dirty slut,' she panted. 'You live on the floor, like a dog, just to get balled.' Genetta felt Marie's thumbs press into her buttocks as she grasped her tightly. 'You're my little bitch, to screw any way I want.' She moved one knee and put it on Genetta's calf, pinning her leg to the floor. 'You whore. You dirty little whore.' She grabbed a handful of Genetta's hair and dragged her head to one side while she pulled the leash to the other. Genetta strained to maintain her position in front of Marie, her hips dipped and her bottom tilted high in the air. More than anything, she knew that she must stay still so Marie could pump her cock in and out of her pussy.

Marie pulled her hair and the leash, and Genetta felt tears welling up from the pain. Her mistress was suspended behind her, and she could picture her, arms bent at the elbows, the veins in her forearms prominent as she held her in an enforced thrall between the Scylla and Charybdis of hair and chain.

Genetta felt the force of Marie's coming; with quick jerks she jammed her hips back and forth. She was moaning, and Genetta knew that her head was thrown back as she was immersed in her own intense orgasm. She swivelled her hips in small tight circles, and Genetta knew she was rubbing her pussy against the vibrating toy, squeezing out of it the last pulses of ecstasy.

'Do you want to come now?' Marie slurred. 'Answer me… do you want to come now?'

Genetta held her breath and nodded vigorously.

'Then you'll have to use an animal, like I just did.' Marie lowered herself to lie down on her back, and instinctively Genetta maintained her position; it was second nature to her now to ensure that her head never rose above the level of Marie's.

'But I don't understand, ma'am,' she said. Even though their faces were inches apart, she respectfully kept her gaze lowered to her mistress's chest.

'Under the bed; there's a present for you,' Marie explained.

'May I get it, ma'am?'

Marie looked up at the ceiling with a smile teasing her lips. 'Yes, I want you to get it.'

Keeping the side of her face on the floor, Genetta slithered over to the bed, and immediately saw the wrapped box. It had a silver ribbon around it that glistened in the afternoon sun cascading through the tall, narrow bedroom windows.

She reached under the bed and dragged out the present. 'A pretty cadeau, all for me,' she said appreciatively, offering a smile in Marie's direction.

Marie made things easier for her by sitting up, so Genetta lifted her head, propped herself on her elbows, and made short work of getting the ribbon and packaging off the box. She lifted the top of the white, damask-printed cardboard expectantly and peered in, and a brown stuffed dog greeted her happy 'Oh!'

'Now ride it,' Marie ordered.

Genetta almost forgot her weeks of training, but stopped herself from looking over at her mistress. 'I beg your pardon, ma'am?'

'Are you deaf today, little puppy? Do you have some congenital problem that the breeder didn't warn me about? Don't make me come over there and cuff you round the head to make your brain work better. Now get on your lovely new doggy present.'

So Genetta did as she was told. She lifted the stuffed animal from the box and manoeuvred it back between her legs. Holding it in place, she began humping it.

'That's the idea. Maybe we'll get some new puppies out of this!'

Marie laughed crudely and Genetta turned her face away. 'Don't you dare,' she said, the threat clear in her tone. Genetta slowly turned back to face Marie, but shut her eyes. 'That's it, puppy, really rub on your cute present. Feel it getting wet from your slit.'

Again, being the obedient servant, Genetta did as she was told. She pushed up on the dog from underneath with her fingers and put the pressure where it was needed.

'Now open your eyes.'

Genetta did so, but kept her gaze averted from Marie's.

'Now look at me.'

The order shocked her. They had worked so hard on getting her to control her eyes, to deny herself the pleasure of gazing at the woman she served. Genetta never even looked at Marie while her owner slept, so she was bewildered for a moment. But the need to look at Marie's face, repressed for seventeen days, asserted itself rigorously.

She flicked her eyes up to her mistress's, and the warmth and pride that emanated from her owner erased any embarrassment Genetta felt at grinding her pussy against the toy between her thighs.

'Come whenever you want,' her mistress permitted.

Genetta sighed deep in her throat and let her eyelids droop as the emergency in her clit heightened. Yet her gaze was still locked with Marie's. She was performing for her, showing her how much she enjoyed being her little puppy.

And melting into this submission, Genetta ran headlong into her orgasm.

With a sharp gasp she felt the rhythm of her grinding turn into the explosion of her sex. She worked her fingers into herself, giving her pussy the friction it needed to jet over the hurdle between her and relief. Her arms ached with the exertion of pressing the dog up against her pelvis. Every muscle in her body was tense. She ground away and humped and regretted the lessening of tension that had to happen every time she drew back from the stuffed animal before she ran her clit against it again.

'Ah... ah,' she groaned, her eyes half shut. The spectre of Marie's amused smile slipped away as her body demanded her full attention. 'I'm coming, I'm coming,' she moaned, and the moan gave way to sighs and gasps of pleasure as the delicious ache of her coming shot through her clit, her pussy, and ended in the clutch and release of her tight, hot tunnel.

She completely collapsed on the floor. The tightness in her arms and stomach receded and the delightful afterglow of gratification made her too lazy to roll off the stuffed dog. The sudden awareness that her eyes were closed caught her, though, and snapped her back to Marie's presence.

'It's all right,' the mistress said, rising and moving to stand over Genetta. 'Don't worry, little girl. You're a well-satisfied bitch right now.'

She rolled over and stretched out at Marie's feet, exposing her body for her mistress's delectation.

'There is one thing left to do, though,' Marie said, and Genetta felt her eyes roam over her until they came to rest on her collar. 'Good dogs clean up the messes they leave behind.'

Understanding implicitly, obediently and without question this time, Genetta rocked herself back onto her side, then up onto her hands and knees. She turned towards the stuffed animal and began licking the spot she had squirmed against.

Forming her hand into a paw by folding her fingers, she stepped on the toy like a real dog holding down a bone, and then she worked over all of the leftover stickiness with broad strokes of her tongue.

'You must be hungry, if that tastes so good to you,' Marie observed.

Genetta understood the compliment Marie was extending to her about her enthusiasm and lifted her mouth long enough to say, 'It's the taste of pussy, ma'am, that I love so much.'

'As do I,' Marie responded. She slid the strap-on down her thighs, pulling the scorpion with it. When the toys lay on the floor, she said, 'All right, let's go get that lunch.'

Marie picked up the leash she'd dropped after screwing her slave. Quickly, Genetta scrambled to heel as they paced out of the room. She practically had to canter beside Marie to keep up, and the mistress did not slacken the speed as they descended the stairs.

When they were in the kitchen Marie dragged her relentlessly around the room as she went from cupboard to refrigerator to microwave.

Some leftover meatloaf and roasted potatoes fell from above into the bowl, which sat on a plastic mat that had the name *Genetta* printed flamboyantly on it.

Genetta dipped her face into the bowl and began taking bites off the chunk of ground beef when her own reflections brought her up short. She was not hesitant to eat because of the presentation of the food and the way she had to go about devouring it. She was grumbling silently about the meal itself! This was a new barrier crossed – when Marie had first led her to the bowl and plopped her food into it, she had cried bitterly at being forced to eat without her hands, dipping her face down into the dog dish. Marie had stood above her silently, and Genetta knew from her failure to tease her that this was very important. Only the act's significance to Marie had made her do it; she did it only to please her mistress.

Now she did it because it was normal – this was the way they shared their meals. She was not as good as Marie was. Mistress ate off the table simply because she was the mistress. Puppy ate from the bowl on the floor because she was Marie's dog. Her pet.

'Eat,' Marie ordered. 'What's the matter with you? Eat, and hurry up.'

Genetta broke off her thoughts and snatched at the food, swallowing it hurriedly. Marie forced her to eat at the pace of a dog, as if she were afraid that someone would come along and steal her food. But Marie always waited until Genetta had licked the bowl clean before taking it away from her.

As Genetta laboured to get the last bite down, Marie spoke. 'Puppy, I'm going upstairs to take a nap. This kitchen is an unholy mess. Clean it while I'm gone.' She kicked the chain out of her way as she left.

Only when she was completely out of sight did Genetta sit back on her haunches and then slowly stand. She had grown so accustomed to moving around on all fours that the soles of her feet tingled when they bore her weight. She knew Marie engineered different times during the day when she could move around naturally – the problem was that upright did not feel correct to her any more.

She sighed as she bent to pick up her bowl and put it in the sink. Life with Marie could be difficult and Genetta admitted that she was not always comfortable in her role, especially at the office. It was difficult not to submit there too, in front of everyone. But Marie was a stern, strict, steady owner, and Genetta felt safe in this house, under Marie's guidance. Again and again during her puppy training, she had become afraid that she was not good enough for Marie. She was sure that there were better, more submissive and deserving women who would suit these complex needs. But as they spent time together, she found that she moulded more and more to the shape that Marie presented for her. Mistress was creating slave in her own image.

She turned on the tap and slowly squirted the washing-up liquid into the sink. Making big, wide, sweeping circles with her hand, she idly made some suds and just as slothfully, washed her doggy bowl.

Then, meandering around the kitchen, lost in thoughts of Marie and the sovereignty Marie held over her, she did her chores.

'Genetta.' Marie's voice sounded from the doorway, and it was firm and stern. Genetta spun to face her, but did not meet her eyes. Marie's feet planted at shoulder's width told Genetta all she needed to know about her mood. 'You are far too slow. Slow, slow, slow.'

Genetta dropped to her knees to accept her inevitable punishment. In one stride Marie was within striking distance, and her palm swept round and landed with a vicious slap against the side of Genetta's face.

She burnt with regret and anguish at her sluggish performance in the kitchen, but more than anything, she felt rage at Marie's audacity in hitting her like that. She stared at a spot right in front of her, something that wasn't her mistress. She knew that Marie looked down into her face and saw her withdrawing from the unfolding scene, and knew what would happen next. Another slap landed on her other cheek, but she remained unmoved.

'You headstrong little bitch,' Marie growled. 'You're not Genetta Macleod, whore-about-town any more. You're not left to your own devices. You have a mistress who demands certain things from you. But every time I tell you to work around my house, you turn into a wretched little slut… and I'm sick of it.'

Marie was serious. Genetta crawled to the dog bed in the corner of the kitchen, near the backdoor, and curled up. She tried to stop herself from shaking, but couldn't.

'If you piss in that bed, I'll hurt you,' Marie threatened. 'If you piss in that bed, I'll mix you up a batch that you won't forget for a long time.'

Genetta hid her face and listened to Marie's steps as she paced the kitchen. She willed her limbs to stop trembling, but her mind was in knots and pain was shooting through her head, neck and back. The more Marie walked the floor, the more Genetta shook and her stomach churned.

'I've had it with you,' Marie announced again. 'How on earth can I train a slave who'll do anything except the dishes?'

She stopped measuring the room in her long strides and Genetta glanced up to see her shake her head in disgust.

'I've tried very hard with you,' the woman went on. 'But I'm sick of your slovenly attempts at obedience. I'm sick of the way you want only pleasure and serve well only when it suits you. You must learn to do what you don't relish, as well, Genetta. It's this refusal to take full part in scenes you don't like that makes you a bad slave. Now get your coat; the puppy training is over.'

Chapter Five

Marie pulled the keys from the ignition and walked around the front of her parked car. Genetta watched her body, her elegant carriage and faultless proportions. If she was a puppy, then Marie was a big cat.

Marie opened her door and Genetta climbed out from the back seat, only to immediately go down on her knees.

'You'll have to stand up to cross the street,' Marie said in an irritated tone, looking around over the car's roof. 'We're in public right now.'

Genetta complied, but said, 'I only want to please, ma'am.' She badly needed to salvage this situation, and she knew it.

'Hm, you should have taken that stance before, slave,' Marie said with evident annoyance. 'It's a little too late now.'

Then, without further ado, she turned on her heel and walked away. Genetta scrambled to stand and move after her, always staying a few feet behind. This was a humiliating situation, but she had brought it on herself, she had to admit. Housework had never been her strong point. But that did not mean it had to be over. She and Marie had been through a lot together; surely it would not end like this.

Marie led her to a storefront door, the glass of which was blackened. It stood unobtrusively in this neighbourhood of nightclubs and gathering places, but Genetta sensed from Marie's anticipation that this was a place well out of the ordinary.

They stepped back together, as if one, when the door began to swing inward and a man emerged. He was tall, and nodded at Marie as he said, 'Good evening, how have you been?' and held the door open for them.

They passed through into a reception area, off which a hallway extended. The lighting was subdued, but clean, and came from some small halogen track-lighting fixtures overhead. The décor was plain. She looked down at the plush, deep emerald-green carpet, and then at the textured ivory walls.

Marie took her money clip from her pocket and unfolded some crisp notes. She handed them to the tall man, who looked at Genetta and said, 'She's not a member yet.'

'No, she's not,' Marie agreed.

'So, is she going to become one?' The man walked to a desk a few feet away and opened a burgundy, leather-bound book that lay on its polished surface.

'I suspect that after tonight she'll be a member in good standing,' Marie confirmed.

'Okay, fair enough.' He took a gold pen from the breast pocket of his blue-and-white pinstriped broadcloth shirt and marked something on the vellum-like page.

He turned towards Genetta and she felt him looking her over. After two weeks of not being allowed to meet Marie's eyes, it was hard for her to look at anyone directly, so she kept her face up but her eyes down.

'She is a cute little one,' he eventually said.

'Stamina, though, she's got lots of stamina,' Marie said proudly. 'And she's got the nerve to be here. I wouldn't bring her otherwise.'

'I believe you,' he said. 'Now give me your coats and go ahead.'

Marie helped Genetta off with her overcoat, then handed it and her own over to the doorman. Genetta stood naked before him, but she didn't relish how he was examining her, and she was glad when Marie beckoned for her to follow.

They approached the nearest door on the right, Marie grasped its brass egg-shaped knob and pushed it, and the honey-coloured oak drifted soundlessly open.

The first things Genetta noted were the pools of lit candles on tables scattered around the room, next to comfortably overstuffed chairs and settees. Clothed men and women reposed on the cushions, while naked others walked to and fro, parading and serving, or knelt at the masters' and mistresses' feet. Everyone looked beautiful in the candlelight.

She gasped faintly.

'Do you feel at home?' Marie asked.

'Yes, ma'am, I think so,' she said uncertainly.

'Very good.' Marie was clearly pleased. 'This is where people like us come to meet other people like us.' She paused, but Genetta could feel that something else was coming – and she was right.

'I'm going to leave you here tonight, Genetta,' the woman went on. 'I'm going to take someone else home with me. You should do the same – go home with someone. You're on your own now.' She kissed Genetta's cheek. 'I've enjoyed owning you, but we've gone as far as we can. I want you to consider yourself released.'

Marie's mini speech stabbed Genetta through her heart, even though she'd been warned. But in spite of herself, she touched her collar; its leather always gave her courage when she felt she was about to be tested. But Marie seemed to sense that she was going to break down, and took

Genetta's hands. Then as a distraction, Genetta thought, and a rather poor one at that, Marie led her on a tour around the room's perimeter.

'This is the lounge area, and kind of a quiet place,' Marie told her in a hushed tone. 'It's a good place to start something, though, because everybody's receptive and watching. Lots of good games begin out here, and then get moved through into the other rooms – where there's proper equipment.'

Genetta squeezed the tears back and glanced sideways at Marie, and she caught a glimpse of her former mistress's encouraging smile. If Marie was going to be this casual about the end of their affair, then so be it. Genetta could be cold, too. She steeled herself as Marie began to speak again.

'Are you not a little curious or frightened as to what that equipment might be?' she asked.

'A little, I suppose, ma'am,' Genetta answered truthfully. 'I guess with all this being new, and with all these people around, then yes, it is a little bit scary.'

'It's okay,' Marie purred. 'I'm glad you can answer me openly. Let's see, I'll make a promise to you, all right?'

'Yes, ma'am.'

'Even though you're no longer my slave, I promise that nobody will strap you down to anything or restrain your limbs in any way this evening. You could take it – I'm pretty well convinced by now that you're a high tolerance submissive – even if a disobedient one.' Marie sighed and shook her head, and Genetta watched her flowing dark hair shine lustrously in the candlelight as it fell around her shoulders. 'But right, you should be initiated slowly into these public pleasures; by your next mistress – or master, I suppose.' She sighed again. 'Anyway, you should take your time; learn what you like and how to get yourself off here. So take things easy and try out many different scenes as time goes by. That's my advice to you.'

'Thank you, ma'am, for considering me.' Genetta made her voice icy and hoped that Marie would absorb the irony.

But she did not seem to. Instead she pressed on, saying, 'I always did think about what you'd like, Genetta. And I'm proud of the brief service you've given me and will always speak fondly of you. Perhaps we'll meet again some day, in other personal circumstances. Our professional relationship at work won't be altered in the least by my sending you away, though; you can rest assured of that. I've taken other girls to bed who've worked for me and never had a problem with any of them.'

'I'm not worried about my job,' Genetta stated defiantly.

'Good, I don't want you to be.'

Genetta saw that Marie had taken up an impenetrable armour along with her decision. Nothing Genetta could say, no subtle dig would make an impression. Marie would never admit how much she might be hurting her.

Marie guided her to a settee. Genetta started to kneel on the floor in anticipation of Marie's sitting, but her former mistress grabbed her wrist and guided her to sit instead.

She found herself looking at the other people in this immediate group, and quickly she dropped her gaze when she realised that she was actually at the top level of the company. All of the submissives and slaves were on the floor, and now that she had taken a privileged place on the furniture, everyone was staring up at her.

And the knowing smiles of the other subs told her that they knew something she did not.

'Sit back,' Marie ordered.

She did so, into the firm support of the cushion behind her.

'Lift your knees.'

Trying not to hesitate or show her misgivings, Genetta lifted her feet off the floor and held her legs suspended in midair.

'Now, spread your legs,' Marie continued. 'Reach down and open your pussy lips. I want everyone to see your delicious jewel.'

Refusing to look at anybody as she performed Marie's wishes, Genetta gingerly reached down to her fringed vulva. She lowered her head a little shamefully as she spread her thighs and pulled her labia wide.

'Go sniff it,' she heard a woman across from her say.

Genetta looked down at herself as a boy-toy clambered to her and pushed his nose against her pussy. He inhaled deeply, withdrew his face, smacked his lips loudly, and then jammed his nose against her again.

His mistress laughed heartily and said, 'Once! You were to sniff it once. And not with so much gusto!' She reached across with a crop and tapped his bottom. He ducked his head and looked up to catch Genetta's eye, smiled and gave her a surreptitious wink, and returned to his place.

Genetta was thankful for the greeting, if a little doubtful about having that mistress use her as a toy for her own slave. Genetta realised that as the newcomer, and in spite of sitting on the settee, she was a tad lower than all of the more experienced submissives here tonight, and that anything could happen.

And the black leather hood Marie produced from a small trunk next to the settee told her that anything would. Genetta watched her from the corner of her eye, until Marie dangled it right in front of her.

'You don't seem to be enjoying yourself, little girl,' she said. 'Maybe it's because you can see what's going on. Maybe if we let you retreat a little from this place, you'll have more fun.'

Genetta obediently nodded her equivocal agreement.

'Very good, now sit up,' Marie ordered.

Genetta did so, but before Marie slipped the hood over her head, she bent down and whispered in her ear. 'Little puppy, I told you that you're released from your servitude to me. You can release Genetta, too. As my slave, she was sometimes modest. But that's not who these people are interested in. They want to see the slave without a mistress. I want the slut in you to come out and show us what she's made of.'

Marie eased the hood over Genetta's head in one deft motion, and as she pulled the cover into place and buckled it, Genetta thought she heard something... something mechanical. Yes – a click of metal encased in plastic, then a low whirr. But those realisations were erased when she was captured by the snug privacy the hood afforded her. What would seem frightening to her in the abstract was actually comforting in practice. She liked how alone she felt. The hood blinded her – there weren't even holes or blinkers where eye slits would be. She now resided in the purest blackness she had ever seen.

The sounds of the room, previously quiet anyway, were now completely gone. And across her mouth, as Marie tightened the buckles, she felt the built in ball gag. It rested just inside her parted lips.

Two small holes let her breath, and there seemed to be a peak in the leather to hold the bridge of her nose.

She was alone, completely alone. She could neither see nor hear anything, so had no way to find out what was going on.

And she felt even more alone when someone – it could only be Marie – loosened the collar from around her throat. Defeated, Genetta bowed her head and felt the leather slip away as it was taken from her.

Marie was right; now she could cut loose. Now she could give control of herself to anyone in this room. The only problem was that she didn't want anyone else.

Someone took her hand in theirs and formed it into a fist. Genetta could tell from the sure, knowledgeable grip that it was Marie. She pulled out Genetta's thumb and turned her arm until her thumb pointed at the floor.

'Safeword,' she heard her say close to the side of her head. 'Safeword. Got it?'

She nodded.

'It has seemed to me, dear Genny, that you've been hungry for cock ever since I've known you. The little incident with the man who screwed your mind out and stole your address book – that little incident that brought us together told me that you were a slut for a hard-on. I thought to change you. But your behaviour with Kate's Daniel the other week let me know that you still want to slide up and down on a rigid prick. Well, my dear girl, tonight's your chance.' And Marie let her hand go.

And Genetta was truly alone.

She shrieked against the ball gag when the rough hands grabbed her ankles and opened her legs. Genetta reached down and pawed, hoping to catch hold of a familiar material or something that would tell her that this was also Marie. This person, though, was naked and male. As he wrestled with her legs she kicked and tried to sit up more. Her fingertips finally brushed what she thought was his chest. It was bare, and devoid of any hair.

But still not entirely sure if she was feeling this man's chest or his back or something else altogether, Genetta continued to fight. Either he didn't understand what she was trying to do or he didn't want to understand, but his grip on her ankles was vicelike. He released her quickly, knocked her shoes off, and then grabbed her rudely again. She sobbed and groaned behind the ball gag, but nothing seemed to stop him.

He pinned her to the settee with his upper body, and Genetta wrapped her arms around him, clawing at his back. But there was nothing else to do. She did not want to safeword and stop the excitement so quickly, knowing that Marie had her in this position because she wanted it – and while Marie might have turned her loose from service, Genetta had to make the transition completely herself. And besides, as the man started butting the head of his cock against her pussy's mouth, Genetta realised that the breathless struggling with him had given her a very hot pulse between her thighs.

So who was he? She might never know.

What did he look like? She could not see.

The only sense she could use to learn about him was touch. Her skin was covered with his impressions – his hands were roving over her, hers over him, his chest was crushing her breasts, her legs were churning against his. She jogged her hips up and down, communicating her desire to him in the only way she could.

From the pressure on either side of her head, against the cushions, she could tell that he was sitting up. Then he had her ankles again and his knees were shoved underneath her bottom.

He placed her feet against him – it must have been his hips, judging from the angles. Holding her ankles there and bending her double at the thighs, he leaned forward. His erect prick pressed against her, but it was too high. So Genetta brought her wet opening up to meet him, and he was in.

He took her roughly. The only connection Genetta had with him was through her captive ankles and feet, and then, through her obedient pussy. She held herself still for him, unable to move anyway because of his tight bondage. Each drive he made into her shoved her down into the wide seat of the settee. He pumped her hard and fast, without any care for her satisfaction. Alone under the nightfall of her hood, Genetta felt her pussy being thoroughly used by a complete stranger.

He withdrew in the same angry fashion with which he had nailed her, dropping her legs and pushing them down roughly. Then another set of strong hands grabbed her shoulders before the other man had fully moved away.

This man put her upright, in a sitting position, then grabbed her legs behind the knees and pulled her to the settee's edge. She spread her legs wide because she knew she was supposed to. It was expected of her tonight. Genetta imagined all the people opposite watching this show. Her passivity during the last balling, she decided, would be in sharp contrast to how she would make herself come this time. She wanted everyone to see her strain and dance on a man's bloated cock.

This next rider was a bit more co-operative than the first. He seemed to have his hands on the back of the settee, so his body was stretched out over and above her.

Blindly, Genetta reached up and found him. Her hands traced over a pair of sinewy shoulders. She ran her fingers down his biceps, following the contours, and then skipped to his flat stomach. She pressed into him there. He was muscular enough, the whole way down to his pelvis, to ensure that she could rub on him and bring herself closer to some remuneration for being the men's fuck-doll tonight.

Before she could let her wandering touch go lower, he centred himself and thrust forward. She grunted behind the ball gag and pushed her tongue against it. His cock was sturdy and of impressive girth. It filled her completely.

He stayed embedded, and instead of pulling away to hump her again, he swivelled his hips. His phallus stayed deep inside, moving in and out in mere centimetres as he ground away at her body.

Genetta reached to his hips and slid her hands over them until she was stroking his buttocks. In response he pulled out a little, then shoved in again.

She locked her calves around his uppermost thighs and began squirming in time with him. Her movements pushed her mound against the lower stomach she had so fervently admired with her hands. His pubic hair wove into hers as she revelled in the friction he created on her clit. She grunted, reduced to only animal-like noises by the gag, and released her legs' clasp on her despoiler. Still he circled his hips lusciously, holding that hard piece of his deep inside her.

Again, Genetta thought of her audience and the spectators in the room. Surely everyone was enthralled by this gangbang. She pictured herself, pinned on the settee and stabbed by this prick. He felt like he had a good body, so the sight of his rotating pelvis and his buttock muscles clenched must have been a very tasty one.

And her own slender body; it must look so pure, bathed in candlelight, so milky against the black leather of the hood. The hood formed her face and head now, and she knew that to her spectators she was less a person and more a body – a body to be enjoyed and used with impunity.

She began driving herself towards orgasm. She rocked her legs back and forth, pushing her clit down against her lover with every one of his measured grinds. Still massaging his bottom, she longed to arch her back and lift herself to kiss him. But all she could do was arch her back. She knew that to the congregation her breasts stood out, as did her ribs, outlined beneath her taut smooth flesh. She threw her head back and moaned, a low, feral, visceral sound. She came for all of them.

And then he was gone, and she took deep, chest-filling breaths through her nose.

Someone else was settling between her legs. Still breathing hard, Genetta opened her thighs for him. He ran his fingers down between her breasts, where she felt the sweat running, and without any more dalliance and without touching her in any other way, he pushed his erection against her. Genetta understood the message and moved until her pussy met his cock, and he slid inside.

Somehow he kept himself from touching her body in any way, and Genetta was too weary to fight him and try for more contact. She lay there, listening to the sounds of her breathing fill her mind while the man outside took her briskly, athletically, perfunctorily.

She swallowed hard and listened. She knew he was still out there, ramming his penis in and out of her, but right now she was more entranced with the sounds in her head. She opened her arms wide and spread them over the settee, then straightened her legs and held her feet up in the air. If he wanted passivity – if anybody watching wanted a torpid, idle slave who was there only to give pleasure with her cunt – then she would give it to him and to them.

Genetta maintained that position as the procession continued. After the third screwing from the athlete who did not choose to touch, Genetta lost count of the number of men who went at her. She was at the end of a line of men who pumped their hard cocks into her, took what they wanted, came in her servile well, and having used her, left her.

Sometimes, when one particular penis suited her, she writhed upon it. Each time that happened she worked her clit up and down a shaft until an orgasm convulsed her insides, colours shot behind her closed eyelids and she was left moaning her pleasure behind the ball gag. It seemed the succession of pricks waiting to get theirs never stopped – would never stop – no matter how she behaved.

But then eventually there were no more. She stayed in her supine position, lest a man come along and find that she was refusing to serve any more. Still, no one came. She listened for a noise, something, anything, but it was no use.

And then fright set in. When the men were mounting her again and again she had not been alone. But now, she was separate. A need to return to Marie's side did not enter her mind – she simply wanted to have somebody near.

Genetta knew that she could get up and walk, but she had no way of seeing where to go. The hood had to come off. When Marie was buckling it around her head it had seemed so intricate and complicated, but no matter what, she had to get out of that hood.

Panic took over. She dragged at the straps that held the ball gag first. With shaking fingers she found the buckles and began grappling with them, but before she could get the first small buckle undone someone came to help.

Quick, proficient, feminine fingers tugged gently at the buckles and released them. The hood was slowly peeled away, and beads of sweat rolled down Genetta's face as the cover was withdrawn.

Chapter Six

She looked around, feeling very much the *ingénue*. As she blinked, a friendly looking young woman leaned down close to her. 'Are you all right?' she asked. Genetta nodded, and the fellow slave went away. Now, Genetta was really on her own.

She knew that Marie would want her to think of herself as an apprentice to the art being practiced in this room, but truly, she had never seen anything like it – nor dreamt it.

All over, on every settee and chair, men and women were having their way with each other. Genetta felt a little abashed; how dare she think that everyone was occupied with her and her acquiescence to getting banged while she lay there like a mannequin? These people were enjoying themselves, not locked inside their own minds with their thought processes shut off. When she and Marie had arrived, there were really only a few people here. Now the room was full, and the men were devoting themselves to the fresh bodies all around.

She ran her fingers over the tender skin beneath her eyes, and then wiped away the beaded sweat on her upper lip. A few tears of mortification, caused both by her own pride and Marie's abandoning her, wetted her lashes. She reached down and brushed her fingertips across Marie's collar. But of course it was gone. Gone.

She stood, a bit unsteady on her feet. Her groin ached from having her legs suspended open for so long. Genetta yearned to find Marie and to be by her side, yet she knew everything between them was now well and truly over.

That meant she could look for someone new, just like Marie was. And this time, she would find a man. Since there was nothing else to be done, she let the thought propel her forward.

Quickly, she walked the perimeter of the room. She had never realised how much the same all naked bodies were – the same, yet different. The men atop the women had their faces distorted with the efforts of their orgasms. The women's taut faces were shielded by the men's backs and shoulders. Genetta watched the male muscles tighten, their hips work as they humped their partners. Even though she had just been ridden by what must have amounted to many of the men in the room, she felt an irascible, white-hot flame of desire quicken in her clit. Some women were standing while men gave them head like mad – those would be the doms, Genetta decided, and she wanted nothing more to do with that. Yet she watched two women making out, one laving the other's breasts with broad strokes of her tongue, and then focussing on the tumescent nipple she'd created. The woman being worked on held her lover between her spread legs and moved her hips. Genetta knew she was rubbing her pussy all over the other woman's stomach. She stopped looking for a new partner for a moment, she was so captivated by the beautiful bodies enthralled with each other.

This was truly orgiastic. Every now and again a smack resounded: the sound of a firm hand hitting pliant flesh. Genetta caught her breath each time, then her eyes darted around to find the couple enjoying a dash of pain with their pleasure.

In the centre of the room a man was reared up behind a

woman, his cock apparently embedded deep within her while he had her long plait wrapped around his fist. His other hand wielded a black leather paddle. He hit her again and again, forcing her to push her bottom back against him in quick, needy thrusts. The woman threw back her head and cried out after one blow and the man shouted, 'Yes! That's it!' He pulled out of her body and pushed her away, though he still had her trapped by her hair. She lunged onto the floor and arched her back, her hands pressed against the mat beneath her, her full firm breasts pushed out into the air, and the man laid into her with a vengeance. He worked her buttocks over with smacks that came at the end of every wide swing he took. Genetta watched his rigid rod between his thighs bounce with each impact. More than anything, she wanted to lower herself in front of him and enjoy his mastery of her and the paddle.

Her eyes followed his weapon in each of its arcs over his head, concentrating on what it must feel like to have a man exercise so much brute control of one's body. She was lost in rapturous thought, and so she jumped, rattled, as something dragged across the flesh of her bare bottom. She tried to turn around, but a hand on her shoulder stopped her. Softly, a man whispered in her ear, 'It's good to see you here, baby. Good to screw you here, too.'

Flustered, Genetta could not respond, and when he pushed against her shoulder in an effort to make her bend over, she felt she had no choice but to comply.

The man stroked her rear, running his hand down over the tender curve and Genetta thrilled at his gentleness, the perfect amount of pressure he applied to the sensitive areas just inside her thighs. He ran the side of his finger into her sex and pushed his thumb against the sensitive region just under her anus.

She tried to concentrate on the lovely way the man attended her body, but her breath was still ragged with excitement from watching that woman get spanked. 'Don't move,' the man said gently, and she felt bad for thinking of someone else while he was being so chivalrous and steady with his touches.

'I'm excited,' she said softly. 'I was just gangbanged, but I want more. I want to feel some pain.'

'I know all that, but pay attention to me.'

'Sorry.'

'That's okay.' He slipped a finger into her dripping pussy. 'You're wet the whole way down your thighs. Did you enjoy playing mattress tonight?'

She smiled a little bit at his joke. 'Yes, most of the time.'

'Do you think you can get this wet on your own?'

'If you keep doing that, we're going to find out pretty soon.'

He chuckled, and she was glad that she'd pleased him.

'Let's just save that test for later, then. Now I'm going to do something different. Steady…'

Genetta bit her lower lip and tightened the muscles in her legs, expecting him to mount her and give her a turn on his cock. Instead, she felt something pushed up into her bottom. She clenched herself without meaning to, and the man gave her a tap on her buttock.

'This is to remind you of your place,' he said. But his tone lacked the seriousness of Marie's when she dominated her. He was being facetious, but delicately so. All the same, Genetta got a feeling he could deal out more serious treatment – and she would not mind being on its receiving end.

He pulled back on her shoulder, and she stood up again.

'Come here,' he said, letting his hand slide down to her hip and wrapping his arm around her waist. She followed his control and stopped when he gave her a light push towards a corner of the room.

'Stand here and don't move,' he said as Genetta looked down at her feet, put her ankles together and then straightened her posture. When she looked up again, she found herself staring at a wall. 'Don't bother looking around if what you see entices you. I don't want you succumbing to the temptation and taking off with another bloke. You've had enough men sweating on you tonight – any more, and I might get jealous. Somebody will be coming for you in a while.'

Then he left her alone. The compulsion to get shagged again took over, and Genetta wanted more than anything to find a man to give it to her and to pump the memories of Marie away. But this man who had just taken control of her – she liked the way he treated her. Seemingly kind but firm – so she would just wait and see.

And wait, she did. She stood obediently, facing the wall, tuning into the sounds of pleasure with her ears, not with her eyes. No one approached her, either. Minutes stretched until, finally, the den of iniquity was clearing out: it seemed the evening was over. Genetta still stood, her forehead pressed into the corner. Once the man had placed her there, it was like she was off limits. Some rule she did not understand had been communicated to everyone that she was reserved for someone's use. Genetta's difficulty lay in the fact that he had not come back to take what he had claimed.

Someone cleared his throat behind her, and Genetta spun to see who it was. Unfortunately, it was the tall man working the door who had blatantly appraised her earlier in the evening, when he let her and Marie into the club.

When she was still with Marie.

Now he looked a little embarrassed by her condition. 'It's over, you know,' he said to her, without meeting her eye.

'I'm aware of that.'

'If you need a cab, I can ring one for you,' he offered.

Genetta stood staring at him, unable to answer. She was shell-shocked; the things that had happened to her… it were as if they had happened to someone else in another time, in another place. Finally she found her voice.

'I suppose it was a good thing I was left out tonight, yeah? Forced to play the wallflower,' she said.

'You can come back another time,' he told her. 'You're a member now.'

'Better luck next time?'

'Something like that.' He glanced at her face and smiled. 'I'll ring the cab for you.'

'It's a shame for me to go home alone,' she said as he backed up a step, but kept looking at her.

'Ah, club policy, I don't get involved with clients, however regular or new they are. It's a shame, really.'

Genetta smiled at his compliment. 'Can't blame me for trying. I do so hate to ride home alone in the evening.'

He grinned this time. 'You have to remember; you were marked by someone for something. Come back another time and see if you can meet up with him again.'

'He mustn't be too interested, or he would've come back to finish what he started.'

'I can't speak for anyone, but maybe you should visit us again. Tonight could all be part of someone's master plan for you.'

Genetta rolled her eyes at his pun. 'Now would be a good time to ring the cab,' she said, smiling at him.

'If you wait here I'll get your coat.'

'Oh yes, thanks.'

Genetta leaned her head against the wall and closed her eyes. She was exhausted from emotional upset, and she was disappointed in herself over her actions – or lack of action – during the astounding events of the evening.

She knew the man had returned when she heard the rustling of material and a quiet cough. Opening her eyes, she saw him hold her coat out, so she stepped forward and allowed him to help her on with it.

He kissed her hair, right over her ear. 'Hope to see you again,' he whispered, and without another word, he took her gently by the elbow and ushered her towards the door.

Genetta gave her address to the cabdriver and back across London they went. It was difficult to fathom how quickly Marie had dropped her; she'd arrived at the club in Marie's car, but her mistress had not even made sure that she had money in her pocket to pay for the cab home.

Chapter Seven

'You've been keeping yourself to yourself these days,' Tracey remarked.

Genetta did not answer, but waited for another observation.

Instead, Tracey examined her cigarette. She tapped it twice with her forefinger, before returning it to her mouth.

Genetta watched Tracey's lips girdle the filter tip and deepen the waxy pink circle already there. As she exhaled, Genetta said, 'It's not very attractive. In practice, you know.'

Tracey finished exhaling the cloud of smoke from her lungs, but her expression changed from noncommittal to puzzled. 'What is not very attractive?' she asked finally.

'Smoking,' Genetta clarified. 'A cigarette can look sexy between some people's lips, but when you inhale, it's all over.'

'Put that in the profound statements file,' Tracey said, rolling her hazel-green eyes. 'What are you doing paying attention to my lips, anyway?'

The sly smile she obviously could not hide around the cigarette made Genetta shuffle her feet and look down, embarrassed.

'That obvious, was it?' she asked quietly. 'Marie and me?'

'I don't know who might have noticed. Nobody talked about it, if that's what you mean.'

'An affair between the dyke boss and one of the office

girls – I'd think every one of you would have had something to say about it.'

'Like I said, I don't know who, if anybody, knows,' Tracey said. 'So, it's over now.'

Genetta noted how Tracey made more of a statement than asked a question, but she didn't think anything more about it.

'Yeah, for a week or so now.'

'So that's why you're keeping yourself to yourself.'

'Yeah.' Suddenly Genetta didn't feel much like talking, so without another word she walked to the door and went back inside to go to her desk.

Marie had given her back her freedom ten days ago, but Genetta had not used it much yet. She had thought long and hard about finding her way to the club this past weekend, perhaps try to find the man who had staked some kind of ownership over her. But the idea of going alone, and having to play at being the bottom for anyone who asked – or demanded – left her cold.

'Hey, Trace,' she said as her friend pulled back her typing chair in the next cubicle.

'Hey, what?' Tracey's head stuck up above the grey burlap wall, and Genetta smiled, knowing that Tracey was standing on tiptoe.

'I was thinking – I've had it with moping about. Want to go out tonight?'

'Like old times? Good idea, Genetta! You need to get out a bit…' Tracey lowered her voice, '…in normal, male company. After all that… mucky business.'

Genetta smiled, determined to be good-natured about the fact that she now had to live down a lesbian affair. 'That was the one and only time for me, believe me,' she vowed. 'It won't be happening again.'

Wearing nothing but a tight black shirt and ankle socks, Genetta rushed around her flat. She threw a pair of close-fitting black trousers over the settee as she cruised by. 'Bloody hellfire,' she muttered. 'Where did my boots get off to?' She opened the door to the tiny hall closet and rummaged around on the floor until she came up with one.

Her make-up and hair were already perfect, she had seen to that. She had to admit, this was quite exciting, to be returning to her old life, and she was taking to it with gusto. But the last month's events still resonated with her. She felt like pleasing herself for a change, that much was true, but she also meant to take things a bit more slowly. Tonight would be the first time she'd gone out dancing since she met that… what was his name… oh, right, that Jack Adams character. What a creep! That was another sort of episode that was not to be repeated.

Genetta nodded ardently to herself as she made up her mind about just what would suit her tonight. A few drinks, lots of dancing, and coming home alone. That was the plan.

She kept digging around for her other boot as she thought. Flinging the first one into the middle of the living room, she sped to her bedroom.

'Aha!' she chortled upon finding the other boot behind the door.

Back out in the living room, she grabbed the trousers from off the couch, then dropped the boot and kicked it until it was next to its mate. Both boots sat near a chair that was in front of a street-side window, across from its mate that was upholstered in a complementary navy blue to the burgundy of this near one.

'Late, late, for a very important date – once again,'

Genetta said, and sat on the chair. 'Oh, bother, forgot the bra,' she muttered. 'And will keep forgetting it tonight.' A giggle escaped her at that thought and she tried to be stern with herself as she tugged the trousers up past her knees. To accomplish the rest of the job of getting them up her thighs, she had to stand.

She lifted her chin quickly as she got to her feet, feeling a few bones in her neck crack as she did so – and something flitted at the window in the flat across the street. It was as if her sudden movements had inspired someone over there to do the same. As if someone were watching her. Responding to her.

And they didn't want her to know it.

All the random thoughts leapt from Genetta's mind and she could do only one thing: hit the deck.

She crawled to the window, which was bare of covering because she'd always liked its oak trim engraved with miniature ivy leaves. Now, she wished more than anything that she'd bought curtains. Slowly, she lifted her head and peeked up over the sill.

Someone was definitely watching. She could see a silhouette behind the sheers that hung between the dark columns of drapery.

'Perv!' she shouted, and pulled herself up to her knees. Staring at the shadow in the flat opposite, she shook a fist and yelled, 'Perv!' one more time for good measure.

She turned and sat down huffily, back against the wall, under the window. 'Wankers,' she growled. 'The entire world is full of wankers all of a sudden. Where have the real men gone?'

Awkwardly, she shoved her hips up into the air and pulled her trousers the rest of the way up. She zipped and buttoned them, then once again on hands and knees, crept across the floor and gathered her boots. 'Where have the *real* men gone?' she asked nobody one more time. 'They've gone off and left us here with sneaky little peeping Toms and thieves and lipstick lesbians.' Tying the second boot with a double knot, she turned back onto her hands and knees and lifted her head above the windowsill, just until she could peek over. The light was off across the way.

'Oh, aren't you clever?' Genetta said scornfully. She stood up then, just to demonstrate for him – it had to be a nasty little 'him' – that he had missed the show. Plucking her purse off the sofa by its strap, she walked quickly through her flat and flicked the light off, opened the door, and left – but not before making sure that everything was locked tight behind her.

'Careers, we've got to think about our careers,' Genetta leaned over and shouted into Tracey's ear. 'Girls like us have got to be able to take care of ourselves. We can't be dependent on anyone!'

Tracey smiled and nodded, but she was staring out at the dance floor and, Genetta knew, not paying her one jot of attention.

'All right then, let's get to it,' she yelled, and then laughed as Tracey jumped out of her chair without a backward glance. Genetta hopped to her feet and followed.

They danced together wantonly, as only two women could. Winding arms, separate, together, above their heads. Standing with legs interlaced and crotches moving inches above each other's legs, they danced.

The two women knew that male eyes were on them as they twirled and gyrated and rolled their bodies against each other. Genetta looked into Tracey's eyes and they both laughed at their pretend lesbianism.

Somewhere in the endless beat of the house music, Tracey caught Genetta's eye again and nodded towards the back of the club. Genetta understood immediately – the loo.

The girls left the dance floor with fingers loosely clasped, as comfortable lovers do on a sunny afternoon's walk. Bodies jostled them, separated them time and again as they made their way.

Bright, white, overhead fluorescent lights in the ladies' contrasted sharply with the musky, blinking dance floor and club. The women's bathroom was a well-lit den dedicated to the pleasures of late night preening. The hairdressing and making-up in here were equal, in intensity at least, to anything in the finest spa – even though the air smelt of stale cigarette smoke and pot while drunken laughter sounded from behind stall doors.

Genetta and Tracey stood in the queue along the wall, waiting to use a toilet or gain a place in front of the long mirror. Each need registered the same importance.

When a pair of girls was done admiring themselves nearby, Tracey elbowed her way to the vacated basin. Genetta clung to her arm and together they found themselves staring at each other's reflections.

'Oh, well done, Trace!' Genetta exclaimed. 'This should cut our toilet time by ages.'

Tracey smiled at Genetta in the mirror, and then bent her head to look down into her small purse. Genetta did the same. In tandem they pulled out compacts, opened them, and proceeded to dust their noses.

'Hot in here,' Tracey said as she examined the ruins of her make-up travelling in rivulets down her forehead.

'Awfully,' replied Genetta.

'Why did we go out tonight again?' Tracey asked, and laughed when Genetta's glance snapped to hers.

'Why? To show me what I left behind when I got involved with… that situation. And to re-introduce me to my normal life.'

'Oh, right,' Tracey said. 'Normal life. Well, here it is, Genny. Exactly as it was when you left it.

'By the way, sorry about not mentioning it sooner, but Paul's coming round later tonight. Any chance you'll want to leave soon so I can get ready for him?'

Genetta smiled knowingly at her friend. 'That's fine, I'm feeling exhausted anyway,' she said. 'He's staying over these days, then?'

'Yes, new development,' Tracey confirmed, 'but we both figured it was time. We've been seeing each other for what feels like aeons, you know.'

'It's been a while,' Genetta agreed. 'Right then, you want to go now?'

'Yes, let's.'

The journey to Tracey's flat took just a few minutes from the club's front door. 'I've always envied how close you live to the action,' Genetta said as they walked together.

'And I've never been able to figure out why you live so far from work and everything else.'

'Maybe I should think of moving closer,' said Genetta.

Tracey glanced sideways at her – Genetta couldn't miss the look – and said with a smile, 'That would be a very good idea.'

They walked up the stairs together, and when they got to Tracey's door, she simply turned the handle and pushed.

'Oh, I didn't think he'd be here already,' Genetta said.

'Um, it's getting late, I figured he would be,' answered

Tracey.

They walked into the flat, which was much like Genetta's and had once been like a second home to her. 'Do you want anything to drink?' she asked Tracey, 'I fancy one for the road.'

'Help yourself,' Tracey said.

'Gin and tonic?' Genetta asked.

'Sounds good,' Tracey said, before calling Paul's name.

Genetta thought she heard some gentle music coming from Tracey's bedroom as she got three glasses down from the kitchen cabinet and found the gin and tonic in the fridge. When she walked back out to the lounge, Paul was sitting with his feet up on the coffee table, arms stretched across the back of the settee. Tracey was nestled against his side, her head resting on his shoulder.

'Here you are,' Genetta said, putting their two drinks on the coffee table, before going back to the kitchen to get her own.

'What a thoughtful maid you are,' Paul said, grinning, when she came back and flopped down in a chair. She threw one leg up over its arm and put her head back in a posture of total ease.

'And that's the last thing I do for anybody tonight,' she sighed wearily, but contentedly. 'I'm knackered.'

'Oh, don't say that, Gen,' Tracey protested softly.

'Why not? It's true,' Genetta said. 'And we have work tomorrow. Going out tonight wasn't the best idea we've ever had.' She glanced at her watch. 'And saying that, I'd better be going in a minute – it's getting late.'

'Genny, we were thinking—' Tracey started before Paul cleared his throat and interrupted her.

'Thinking what?' Genetta asked, lifting her head and staring at both of them.

Paul took a big breath, and then he looked at Tracey. She stared deeply into his eyes, and then nodded in an encouraging way.

'You have to be frustrated,' said Paul, looking over to Genetta.

'It has to have bothered you,' Tracey added.

'And we want to help,' Paul said, with an attitude that he'd said everything that needed saying.

'What?' Genetta asked, unsure of this sudden twist in the conversation. 'You want to help with what?'

Paul sighed, and then pulled his arm up and over Tracey's head and took his feet off the table. Leaning forward, elbows on knees, he concentrated a stare on Genetta.

'Tracey told me about your recent relationship with your boss,' he said, 'and neither of us had ever suspected that you might be into women as well as men.'

'Where are we going with this?' Genetta asked in a subdued tone, hypnotised by the gin and the cadence of Paul's smooth voice.

'All right, to put it bluntly.' He cleared his throat. 'I fancy you, Genny – we both do.'

Genetta looked down at the dewy glasses sitting on the table. She licked her lips slowly, then pursed them for a second, unsure how to proceed. 'Is this for real?' she eventually asked, and looked across at Tracey.

Her friend met her gaze with a level look, and her hazel eyes looked as if a fire smouldered behind them.

'Take out your frustrations with Paul,' Tracey urged. 'Go on, I want to watch him give you everything he's got.'

'I'm sure he's got a lot,' Genetta said, but she shook her head. 'This isn't on, you two. It's just not on. There'll be nothing but trouble over this later between you and me, Trace. I know it – trust me.'

'Why don't you let us worry about the future and everybody's relationships with everyone else?' Paul asked.

'Because the future's not really between you and me, Paul,' Genetta responded. 'It's my friendship with Trace that is important. That's what worries me.'

Tracey stood and began tugging her tight white blouse out of the little plaid schoolgirl skirt she usually wore to the clubs. Paul cast an appreciative glance at her breasts, and then looked at Genetta again. She, in turn, watched Tracey's actions, then met Paul's dark stare.

'Just watching another girl get undressed isn't going to turn me on,' she insisted flatly. 'Not after what I've been through.'

'Maybe not,' Paul conceded, 'but I'd be surprised if watching what I do to her after she's undressed doesn't.'

And Genetta had to admit to herself, she already felt the quickening in her clit at the mere thought of watching the two of them together. 'My own private sex show?' she mused.

'All for you,' said Paul.

In the meantime, Tracey had slunk out of her skirt and socks and shoes. Paul reached out and grabbed her by the waist. She fell backwards onto his lap and Genetta watched him push his hips up to meet her bottom.

He wasted no time, but pushed his fingers under the waistband of Tracey's panties. She lifted herself enough for him to slide them down her thighs, and then she pushed them past her knees and kicked them off. Paul pulled her back against his chest and Genetta gasped as he began kissing and suckling the side of Tracey's throat.

Tracey arched her back against him, rubbing her shoulders on his chest. She lifted her rear and Paul reached under her to loosen his jeans and unzip them.

Genetta's breathing got heavier as he slid his hands up Tracey's sides and cupped a full breast in each hand. His lips and mouth continued their work on her neck, and he added gentle twists and tweaks on Tracey's nipples.

Tracey slid forward a little on his legs and reached beneath herself. She was fumbling with his jeans.

Becoming more and more involved in what they were doing, Genetta dropped to her knees and crawled to the couple. She ran her fingertips over Paul's hands as they cupped her friend's breasts, and shut her eyes as she felt his knuckles and encompassed his broad wrists. Then she reached under Tracey's straining body and felt for his hardness.

It was easy to find, and she pulled his jeans down a bit more, then his pants. She could just see the vermilion head of his cock peeking out, and with another gentle tug she eased the elastic down over his prick and balls.

'Oh God,' he groaned as she thumbed the dripping end of his cock and squeezed the shaft. When she slipped her palm up, pulling his foreskin in her grip, more pre-come leaked out and ran down over her fingers.

Genetta pushed the tip of his glans into the valley of Tracey's bare bottom, and a soft grunt sounded from Tracey's throat as the slippery end of Paul's penis nudged against her.

'I want it against my clit,' Tracey moaned. She reached down between her legs from the front and Genetta felt her fingers, too, on Paul's hard length.

'Don't know if I can control myself long enough,' Paul groaned lustily.

'You'll have to,' Tracey said, and Genetta smiled at seeing her friend get so bossy when she was horny.

'See, Gen,' Paul said, and Genetta turned her gaze from his swollen prick to his dark eyes. 'Tracey likes to play a game with my cock. She likes to sit like this and take it against her slit. And she slides up and down and teases herself and rubs her clit on my shaft until she comes and comes and comes. Only then do I get to fuck her properly.'

'Sounds like a fun game,' Genetta said softly. She loosened her grip on his erection and trailed her fingers along it as Tracey pulled it into her wetness.

'You can play with it first,' Paul said, grinding his hips up.

'I don't mind watching Tracey play,' she said. 'And I'll play by myself while I do.'

She held Paul's gaze steadily as she rocked onto her bottom and untied her boots. After she kicked them off, she pulled her black trousers down and slid out of them, too.

'No panties?' Paul asked.

Genetta shook her head mischievously.

'No bra, either?'

She shook her head again, her eyes sparkling as she warmed to the increasingly exciting atmosphere in the room.

'Oh,' he groaned as Tracey moved seductively on top of him, and Tracey groaned with him, and Genetta could take no more.

She pushed three fingers between her thighs and panted to feel how wet she was. She was up for this excitement, even more than she'd realised when she caught the first glimpse of Paul's erection – and now she was boiling over. She rocked up onto her knees and crawled to a better vantage point, right in front of Tracey and Paul. Tracey's legs were shut tight around his cock, but Genetta could see that delectable head peek out from Tracey's dark pussy hair. It was true – Tracey was holding his length against her, sliding on him, using him like a dildo to masturbate herself.

Genetta kept her three fingers tightly together and jerked her hips so that her pussy moved against her steady hand. She looked up from Tracey's sex and saw Paul watching her.

'I need to be fucked,' she said softly.

'I know you do,' he answered, in tones just as sultry and low.

'Talk and I'll come,' Tracey cried out.

'I need a hard pole shoved up into me,' Genetta sighed. 'All I want is a man on top of me and inside me. I'm wet, Tracey. I want Paul to ride me and treat me like a whore. I want to suck the come out of his cock and lick his balls until he's hard again and then stab myself down onto his stiff rod until I come again.'

And Tracey came. With her eyes misty with lust, Genetta watched her friend begin to shake. Tracey arched her back, her nipples stood at attention and her thighs quivered inside the tight grasp of Paul's legs. A red flush spread over her chest, down onto her breasts. And still she shook.

Genetta collapsed on her back. 'Come here and give it to me,' she whispered to Paul, then spread her pussy lips wide and masturbated for him, knowing he still watched her. She stretched her fingers apart, flattening her pouting labia while she flicked her tumescent, begging clit with her middle finger.

A few minutes went by and Genetta pushed herself closer and closer to the edge of release. Her empty pussy begged to be filled, but her aching button wanted to explode under her own touch. 'Paul, please,' she begged.

'It's too uncomfortable on the floor,' Paul said from right above her. Genetta opened her eyes to see him standing, looking down at her. 'Let's go to the bedroom.'

'Yes please,' she whispered. She knew how good it was going to be with him, but it was only reluctantly that she pulled her hand away from her wetness and the throb that needed more attention.

Quickly, Paul took her hand, wet with her juices, and pulled her to her feet. 'Come on, I need you,' he said.

'But she needs to remember her place, Paul,' Tracey said. 'You know that. I told you.'

Genetta turned to see her friend standing in her naked glory, her hazel eyes intense with something that now looked less than lust, and more like a desire to control.

'Tracey, I had no idea you were into…' Genetta began, her voice tailing away when she saw what Tracey produced from behind her back.

It was the collar.

It was the collar Genetta had worn to show her submission to her mistress. The collar Marie had finally taken from her at the orgy.

Tracey now held it, and Genetta's uncertain glance flickered from her to Paul and back again.

'I just happened to mention to Marie that you'd be coming here for a little fun with me and my man,' Tracey explained confidently. 'And she recommended that I have you wear this so you'll remember he isn't yours. So you'll remember you're below me, that I can punish you for being naughty or pushy or demanding. Or for any reason I choose, really.'

'But, Tracey…' Genetta began, but there was absolutely nothing to say. She wanted to know everything – how Tracey had gotten the collar, what exactly Tracey knew about the rules of the relationship with Marie, if Tracey knew everything else about Genetta's world over the past few weeks – but there was no reason to ask those questions.

Because Genetta already knew the answers.

'Take her through to the bedroom,' Tracey said to Paul. 'We're going to give her the fucking she craves, all right.'

Genetta looked to him, and Paul gave her an amused but sultry look. He looked like he thought it was all playacting. But if Tracey had learnt from Marie, Genetta knew that very little play was going to be involved.

Wearing nothing but her ankle socks and blouse, Genetta walked in front of Paul. She knew where the bedroom was, and she knew there was absolutely no going back now.

She squirmed a little when she sat down and felt the rubber sheet on the bed. She sat at the very edge, trying not to notice what might be a portent of the antics that Tracey had in mind for her.

She and Paul were alone for a moment. 'This is all a bit of a shock for me, Paul,' she said. 'To hear that Tracey knows a lot more about my relationship with Marie than she's ever let on. It just makes me wonder—'

'Makes you wonder who else has been one of Marie's girls?' Tracey asked, sauntering into the bedroom, holding an ice bucket with a bottle in it. Casually, she placed the bucket on the bedside cabinet.

'I – I just thought we were going to enjoy ourselves together, the three of us,' Genetta said, feeling increasingly uneasy.

'Oh, you're going to enjoy yourself, Genny, don't worry. I'm not into the whole humiliation trip that Marie likes to take. I learnt that by crawling around on the end of her leash.'

Genetta cowered in front of that statement, as much as she'd shrunk inside herself when she saw the way the bed was kitted out. For someone who wasn't into humiliation, it seemed Tracey knew how to dish it out.

The two girls stared at each other, hazel-green eyes bearing down into Genetta. 'Move your hair away,' Tracey ordered, and Genetta did as she was told as Tracey fastened the black leather band around her throat.

'Take your clothes off and get on the bed,' Tracey instructed Paul, and he instantly complied.

Kneeling on the bed, his erection standing proud between his thighs, he put his hands on Genetta's shoulders and pushed her down gently. She fell back under the pressure and raised her face to his as he leant down to kiss her.

The stubble on his chin rasped against her soft complexion, and the hardness of his mouth, the strength of his jaw, was remarkable. Paul's mouth felt so new to her after weeks with Marie; it was as if she had never kissed a man before.

She wrapped her arms around his shoulders and marvelled at the latent potency of him. Had men always felt so good – so raw? For the first time in a long time, Genetta felt inexperienced with the male body.

Her hands slid down his biceps, onto his forearms as he held himself above her and laved her tongue with his. Genetta's instincts ruled when presented with such masculinity and she spread her legs, inviting him in. His reflexes were ruling him too, and his rigid cock began inching into her vagina.

'Paul,' Tracey said softly. 'We have other plans.'

Her voice seemed to call him to his senses – much to Genetta's vexation. 'What other plans?' she asked, wresting her mouth from his, but digging her fingers into his arms and refusing to let go.

He smiled down at her, his dark brown eyes indicating affection. 'Just other plans,' he said. 'Yours isn't to ask...'

'I know, it is to perform,' she said.

'No, it's not necessarily like that at all. We just want you to let us enjoy you. And in the process, enjoy yourself. Isn't that what being submissive is all about?'

'At this moment I don't know anything about submission,' she said. 'All I know is that having you on top of me is the best feeling I've had in a long time.'

'Do you want that full feeling that only a man can give?' Tracey asked, lying down beside her.

Genetta looked at her friend and examined her face for signs of deception or teasing – and did not see any. 'Yes, I do,' she whispered honestly. 'I've missed making love to a man.'

'Then that's what you'll have,' Tracey declared. 'Like I said, Gen, I'm not into Marie's scene – all that mistress and slave playacting. I just want to make you feel good, and to make us feel good, too. Paul and I want this to bring us closer by letting us get to know each other's sexuality more.'

'Okay, that sounds good,' Genetta said. 'No matter how you explain it, you're both using me for your own ends. But that's all right, so long as I get to enjoy myself too.'

'Oh, you'll get to enjoy plenty,' Paul insisted, and Tracey smiled and nodded her agreement.

He kissed Genetta and rolled off her, then trailed his hand down her thigh as he got off the bed. He walked around it, picked up the ice bucket, and handed it to Tracey after taking the bottle of beer out.

'Go on then, Trace,' he said, 'feed some into her.'

Genetta watched as yet again the dominant role shifted effortlessly between male and female. Now, once again being under Paul's control inflamed her temperature, and she instinctively understood what he wanted. She pulled her thighs back, her hands behind her knees, comfortable now with the necessity of the rubber sheet; it was there to stop the mattress from getting wet as the ice cubes melted and water seeped from her as Paul and Tracey did things to her tight, yearning pussy.

He stood there, drinking the beer, watching Tracey, and Genetta turned her attention to her friend as well. Tracey took some of the smooth ice cubes and ran them down the junction of thigh and pussy lip on one side, and then the other. The secret skin there tingled, and the dripping water ran down between the cheeks of her bottom.

'Does that feel good?' Paul asked.

'It feels a little funny,' Genetta admitted, and gazed up at him with a smile.

Tracey stroked Genetta's clit with her knuckle a few times, then slipped the ice cubes back to her opening and pushed them in with her thumb. Genetta sighed as Tracey got more ice and pushed it into her the same way.

Slowly, Genetta's insides went cold, then numb. She could not feel the pressure of Tracey's thumb any more, nor could she even tell how much ice was already inside her. But the outer areas of her sex – her clit, especially, which was well out of the freezing action – retained its feeling, and fervour.

Tracey moved away and Paul took her place between Genetta's legs. He laid his arm across her belly, and at the same time took a long lick over her nub. Genetta gasped at the difference between the cold of the ice and the warmth of his mouth.

With one steady push, he eased the beer bottle inside. The glass scraped against the protrusions of ice inside her and Genetta clenched her teeth against the paradoxical sensation.

She raised her head to look down at Paul, and he was watching the bottle go in and out of her with a discerning eye, as if he'd seen a lot of things travel into a woman's body and enjoyed every sight. Even though the unyielding glass pushed the ice against her vaginal walls, and she could feel that discomfort, Genetta let him have his way; he clearly enjoyed what he was doing.

She felt the mattress give, and looked to see Tracey moving to join Paul at her parted legs.

'That looks so sexy,' Tracey murmured after a few moments of watching the bottle penetrate Genetta. 'The delicious sight of her makes me so hot.'

'And what would you like to do about that?' asked Paul.

'Well, I'd love to come,' Tracey suggested mischievously.

'Hmm... I thought you might say that,' he mused.

Genetta looked down at the pair and saw Tracey gazing hungrily at her. 'You've such a pretty mouth,' Tracey purred, and then came slinking up the bed.

Genetta opened her mouth and tilted her head back; her lips eagerly ready to accept Tracey's turgid sex. And Tracey did not disappoint her. She straddled Genetta's face and settled her wet pussy down.

Although Genetta had performed this act many enjoyable times before, with Marie, this was the first time she had ever eaten a pussy without feeling subordinate.

She probed into Tracey's secret cavern. It tasted just a tiny bit of a man's saltiness; so earlier Paul had managed a surreptitious penetration once or twice, she thought.

She would have smiled, had Tracey not been grinding her insatiable clit against her lips.

Genetta took that bud firmly in her mouth and began flicking her tongue against it. She knew the rapid speed that another woman needed, the way to cause vibrations between someone else's legs. A guttural moan escaped Tracey's throat and let Genetta know that she was working it at just the right tempo.

'Make her into your whore,' Paul encouraged, and at first Genetta wasn't sure which one of them he was talking to, but when he continued, 'it's my turn to make her into mine now,' she knew for certain that he meant her.

The name-calling turned her on. He was kneeling between her parted legs and she rubbed the insides of her thighs against the hairy outsides of his, then up to his slim hips, all the while concentrating on the succulent centre of Tracey's pleasure.

But the instant Paul sank his erection to the hilt with one controlled stroke, Genetta's devotion to Tracey's pleasure were over – forgotten. Now she wanted only to think about her own orgasm, and how she would get it from the rigid stalk of flesh Paul was pumping in and out of her.

And he had picked the perfect moment. The freezing effects of the ice were almost gone, and the narrow bottleneck had proved to be a pretty poor dildo, but his cock – so hard, so tightly stretched and turgid – was perfect. It reached up towards her womb, where she needed him to be.

Tracey was moaning more and more urgently. Hurriedly, Genetta licked and sucked and nibbled and teased her clit, doing anything it took to take Tracey all the way. Paul was driving in and out of her, pursuing his own ecstasy.

As hard as she could, Genetta worked her hips up and down against him, but Tracey's weight was holding her back and she could not get Paul's cock to penetrate her at the right angle.

Then Tracey came. Genetta felt the pulse against her chin, the tightening of Tracey's opening that signalled how her insides were constricting and squeezing, over and over again with her climax.

And Tracey seemed to sense what Genetta needed. She dismounted her face quickly and took Genetta's breast in her mouth and suckled at her nipple relentlessly.

The sensations were too much. Genetta wrapped her fists in the sheet that was crumpled under her and pulled. Tension built in her from Paul's thrusting, from the way she rocked her hips against him and felt the base of his cock pressing and rasping on her clitoris. The shaft of his prick never left contact with her little erection now. With a blaze of colour behind her closed eyelids, Genetta exploded on Paul's large, demanding erection.

As she resurfaced she felt him shoving his hands under her hips, so she kept moving her sex along his length, and with a grunt and a sigh against her shoulder, he came too.

He rolled off her, his passion spent. When he was finished, Tracey was too. Genetta looked down to see her friend lift her face from the nipple she'd been avidly suckling.

'Oh!' she exclaimed.

'What's the matter?' Tracey said sweetly, innocently.

'What did you do?' Genetta said, pulling her breast to see the mark more clearly. 'That's a love bite!'

Paul shifted onto his side and strained for a second to see the mark. 'You're branded,' he said, looking at Genetta with a sly smile. 'Branded as a submissive little whore.'

Chapter Eight

He could not resist any more. The sight of his slave's red bottom must have proved too much for his self-restraint because he grabbed her ponytail and dragged her backwards, off his lap. She fell to her knees beside him, and the spectators heard the ragged sobs that wrenched themselves from the spanked girl's throat.

Genetta turned slowly and walked around the pair, savouring the changing perspective of their bodies. He was the master of the proceedings, and Genetta liked him. She liked his casual look, shirtless and blue jeans, in a world where costume was *de rigueur*. He was pared right down to raw masculinity with no façade. Only his actions and the muscle behind them declared his dominance.

With an eye equally practiced at appreciating the female form, Genetta surveyed the submissive who made the less-than part of this living equation. A cowgirl, complete with black and white cowhide waistcoat that had a buckle at the back, drawn tight to reveal the hourglass of her waist. When she had been over her master's lap, her breasts swayed invitingly down beside his thigh.

But her bottom, reddened and chastised as it appeared, was the most charming thing about her, for she wore a pair of black leather riding chaps that exposed each cheek like a portrait in a frame. Two portraits of blushing, rounded buttock flesh.

Right below her spanked posterior, the leg on each portion of the chaps was tied with leather straps. The backs of her thighs peeked through, as white as her abused bottom had no doubt once been.

The contrast of black leather on red skin then white was eye-catching. Even though she had been the willing little slut bent over to take her punishment in the past – and it had hurt – Genetta was turned on to see flaming skin from a top's perspective.

That was as close to topping as Genetta wanted to get tonight, however. She had wheedled her way in here, sweet-talking the doorman and flirting until he acquiesced…

'…I gave a lot of your members a good time, didn't I? And I know you peeked in and watched. The couch I was spread on while they gave it to me, one after the other – you can see it from the doorway. I know you watched me. You saw me being fucked by cock after cock, I know you did…'

Genetta smiled to herself, recollecting the monologue she had given in a low, seductive voice, bent over his little writing table, dangling her breasts over his guest book, letting him know she was naked underneath her coat. He worked the front of the club, looked all the women over in an unassuming but appreciative way – he had to be a voyeur. So she'd painted a vivid word picture for him and he had responded by writing her name down in that precious book with a shaky hand, and letting her in without making her pay.

He clearly wanted her, that much was obvious. And it had been fun, using her sexuality as an incentive for him to break the rules a little bit.

But Genetta was here tonight for one thing: a man who could take her in hand. She didn't want to be looked at. She wanted to be used.

More words echoed in her mind as she watched the spanked slave show off another skill – her cock worship.

Paul and Tracey were right; Genetta was a submissive whore. The dalliance with Marie, the experience of the lesbian world – it wasn't really her. Having her pussy eaten, being screwed with a strap-on were all right when that's all she could get. But nothing about another woman turned her on the way she dripped with wetness when her fingers encircled a cock that was so hard it was ready to burst. And when the head of a solid prick butted against her, ready to penetrate, only then was Genetta on the road to complete satisfaction.

A man. She wanted and needed a man. One who knew how to play rough. She needed a master to take her in and abuse her like the commonest of sluts. She wanted to be enslaved.

Watching the spanked girl rub her master's hard-on, glistening with pre-come, all over her face, made Genetta ache with desire. She had to move in order to hunt.

In the rest of this dungeon room the same panoply of sexual excess was happening. Naked flesh, heaving chests, tense faces. The sounds of floggers hitting bare backs – an unmistakable sound to Genetta after only one experience – and martinets cracking and wooden paddles slapping, all employed to do the business. Women on women, men on women, women on men. Where was the man Genetta sought? And if she couldn't find him, at least not this very night, then where could she fit in?

A sudden stabbing glare of light caught her attention, and she squinted towards its source – a rather large mirror that a male slave was clearly having trouble holding.

No one else looked like paying attention to his problem, so although she was well across the room from him, she walked over, weaving among sprawled, humping, copulating bodies, and took a side of the bothersome mirror.

The slave smiled his thanks at her and she looked him over. He was sinewy, but fairly thin. She narrowed her eyes to regard him closely – had he been one of the men who'd gangbanged her? She stared at his face. No, she sensed he hadn't been.

'Why are you holding this thing?' she asked when their eyes met. 'Because you're a slave?'

'Of course,' he answered, with a little chuckle in his voice. 'Really, my mistress and I are friends with this couple.' He nodded his head and Genetta looked to where he indicated. 'So she offered my services to make sure they have an interesting night.'

A woman – the bottom, literally, thought Genetta – was lying on her back on a dais. Her ankles were caught in binds and a short black length of webbing ran behind her neck, connecting ankle to ankle. The webbing lead was short, drawing her knees back to her shoulders, but she clearly enjoyed having them lifted and spread open like that.

With her hips on the platform's edge, her position exposed her entire underside to anyone and everyone. And inserted into her bottom, held there by her own muscular control, was a pliable purple dildo.

As the master eased it in and drew it out, Genetta could see it was specially suited for its task. Its tip was pointed and narrow and it had a sculpted look where it curved in to a quite thin indentation before it curved back out to get wider. From that point on, it grew wider and thicker, all the way back to the base. The master held it between his fingertips and thumb and eased it in and out of his whimpering slave's bottom.

'Does it feel good, do you think?' Genetta asked her new slave acquaintance.

'I suspect it feels fantastic,' he said impishly. 'And it's pretty clear she gets something out of it.'

Genetta smiled and nodded knowingly, as if she understood all of the rules of the game. But her imagination was captivated by the goings-on in front of her. 'Can you hold this thing yourself now?' she asked him.

The young slave leaned forward and looked around the mirror at someone. Genetta turned her head as far as she could and saw a blonde woman, spread-eagled on a chair, entwine her fingers in the short dark hair of a man who was suckling her full breasts. She put a finger to his lips, said a few words, and he nodded before rising to his feet. 'Yeah, okay,' the slave said, 'we can put it down now.'

'Your mistress?' Genetta asked, turning to look at him again.

'Oh yes, she's my mistress,' he said, and she could hear the pride register in his voice.

'That's wonderful; that the two of you have such a connection. That looked close to telepathy to me.'

'It was.' He smiled broadly and raised his eyebrows as he glanced over her shoulder. Genetta turned and looked up at the man who had just been adoring the mistress's breasts, his lips glistening wetly from savouring her nipples.

Genetta was incredibly turned on. When she had asked the slave to hold the mirror himself again, she had been caught up in a wild idea. Now she knew that she would follow through to its fruition – whatever that might be.

She moved to the dais upon which lay the bound, exposed slave. Letting her eyes travel over the woman's haunches, across her parted thighs, down to her gently penetrated bottom, Genetta made her way to the master in charge.

'Hello,' she said, keeping her gaze pinned respectfully to the centre of his chest. 'Can you explain to me what's happening here please, sir?'

'A slightly different kind of pleasuring,' he said, after a pause in which he seemed to look Genetta over and assess the variables she might present.

'I've never gone in much for anal play,' Genetta said in a quiet tone, as if admitting to something very naughty.

'You've not been brought to it correctly, then,' he stated. 'If you'd been introduced to the... luxury, of having your bottom treated well, you would be devoted to this, just like my little whore here.' He indicated the woman bound on the dais.

Genetta watched the slave's anus distend around the purple toy. 'I can see that she enjoys it, sir, but what do you get out of it?'

'I get the pleasure of having a completely turned-on submissive,' he told her. 'She can't achieve a satisfactory orgasm this way, so she's teased and left in a state of delicious frustration while her bottom is tormented until I decide otherwise.'

'And then what happens?' Genetta asked.

'And then, when I decide she's had enough, she's more than willing to do anything I demand,' he answered frankly.

Genetta stood still as they fell into silence together, and he scrutinised her naked beauty closely. His gaze crawled over her body for long tense seconds, and finally settled on the one thing she still wore.

It was a long necklace. Round, brick-red jasper beads hung down over her breasts and looped back up to her neck, where she had doubled the necklace's coils and it encircled her throat, forming a choker.

This was all she had worn to the club: her black leather coat – now with the doorman – and the jasper necklace. One covered everything, the other nothing. The first sufficed to get her to the club and in the front door. The second was helping her to make her way even now because the necklace pretended to hide her charms, acted as if it wanted to clothe her... but could not. The result, Genetta knew, was electrifying.

The master surveying her was responding to the necklace's invitation to come closer and see what it failed to hide. His nostrils flared and his lips tightened for a moment – he really wanted her, Genetta could tell. Undoubtedly, he had to have her.

And so she ventured to speak. 'The problem, sir, is that I don't have a master who would initiate me into this kind of undoubted pleasure.'

'You don't have a master?' he echoed, his interest clear.

Genetta nibbled her lower lip, for two reasons: firstly, because she knew it looked innocently becoming, and secondly, to stop herself giggling at the master's awestruck tone. She could get used to not being owned if it meant she could come to the club, talk with whomever she chose, and engage in whatever playtime activities presented themselves.

'I had a mistress,' she went on, by way of explanation, after allowing him to absorb the reality that she was alone. 'But she, um, turned me loose. And now I'm a loose submissive.'

'And we like that one kind of loose,' he said. 'But you don't sound too happy that she let you go.'

Genetta looked into the master's blue-grey eyes and

took a deep breath while she considered her answer. 'Let's just say that she introduced me to this world of dominance and humiliation, let me develop a taste for it, then brought me here one night to get rid of me.

'And I've taken a few lumps since then,' she went on, liking the way the master appeared interested, 'not knowing my way around and not having someone to help me. And I tried to take up my pre-scene life again. But I can't leave this new realm behind me. Somehow, some way, the people involved in all of this have got a hold of me. And they aren't going to let me go, it seems. So my problem is that I want to find a man to keep me and teach me and train me, and who'll let me come here to enjoy the things I like, as well.'

'A man?' the master pressed. 'So what's wrong with having a woman continue your training?'

'I'd prefer it to be a man,' Genetta insisted, and then turned her attention more fully to what he was doing. All the while they'd been talking he had been moving the dildo in and out of his slave's bottom, rhythmically and slowly. It was obviously something that gave both top and bottom a great deal of pleasure, and they must have done it often – so often that the motions and speed were as natural to the master as was his own breathing.

Genetta lowered her eyes to watch a little more closely.

The light from a recessed fixture overhead cast a soft, warm, golden glow over the slave spread out on the dais. It all looked very sensual, but Genetta's favourite part was something that was rather difficult to see. The slave was so wet her pussy juices were coating her perineum. Genetta could see how her vaginal lips glistened with her wetness as well, closely shaven as they were.

She was utterly transfixed by the lewd sight. Every now

and again the slave shuddered and her pussy spasmed. 'I'm wet, too,' Genetta said in a low whisper, not really caring whether anyone heard her or not.

'Then you may use my slave,' the master responded. 'You've been with a woman before, so let's not be shy now.'

Genetta turned and looked at him. His wolfish eyes were glowing hot with desire and intent.

'Will that make me submissive to both of you, or just you?' she asked, wanting to ensure that the power plays were negotiated before she began to enjoy herself. And oh, how she would enjoy herself.

'Just me,' he confirmed, smiling slyly. 'Plus, of course, any other master I care to invite to join us.'

Genetta smiled.

'Indulge yourself on my slut's face,' the master said.

Genetta took a few paces until she was at the slave's head. The other woman did not even look up at her. She simply opened her mouth, stuck out her tongue, and began working it in the air.

Genetta understood that she was to make use of that swirling pink action, but she turned first to the young slave who had held the mirror. 'I want to watch myself come,' she said to him, and his mistress, who was watching events unfold with interest.

'Tell us what your fantasy is,' he said to her, the mischief gone from his voice and expression, 'and we'll do what we can to make it come true.'

'I – I want to be fucked every way possible,' she stated brazenly, even surprising herself with her forwardness. 'And I want to watch the whole delicious thing while it happens.'

'Then that is what you shall have, miss,' the young

slave said. He stared into her eyes and Genetta returned his gaze for a long second, before looking at his chest and stomach, down to the sight of his bare prick. It was stirring, lengthening, growing under the scrub of black hair above it.

'Mm, perhaps I'll get everything I want,' she said impishly, then turned her back on him before he could answer and put her palms flat on the platform of the dais, on either side of the bound woman's head. With a little push and jump she was kneeling there, and then she eased her swollen, greedy clit down to that gyrating tongue.

A stab of pure sexual satisfaction shot through her body. She purred as she dug her fingers into the slave's hair and positioned her just as she wanted her. By now, thanks to the diligent attentions of Marie, Genetta knew exactly what she liked.

But the slave seemed to have other ideas. She spread the cheeks of Genetta's bottom, and while her hands were still back there, she began pushing Genetta up over her face. Genetta fought against it until she realised what was happening; the woman wanted to rim her.

Fair enough, she thought, and gave in to the new pressure.

When the slave's tongue first probed her entrance Genetta instinctively licked her lips. It was a reflexive action that indicated just how delectable the rimming felt, how exquisite it was to have a pointed, wet, velvety tongue prodding just inside her bottom. The slave circled the outside of the hole, up between Genetta's cheeks, over and over, and then stabbed inwards again – and again the tip of Genetta's tongue emerged in response.

Then the dais under her shimmied a little and seemed unstable for a moment. Genetta opened her eyes, slightly annoyed that her blissful moment was being interrupted.

She looked over her shoulder and there was the master. He cupped her buttocks as well, and began guiding her hips around in circles over his slave's mouth.

Genetta could barely see straight, she was so overwhelmed with pleasure, but she managed to catch the eye of the slave holding the mirror, and direct him. He and his mistress stepped back a bit and let the whole of the debauched scene appear in the mirror, so when Genetta looked to her side she saw herself, writhing wantonly on her knees over the slave's face. The master had freed his slave's ankles and allowed her to straighten her legs flat, and was kneeling astride her, his balls dangling across her breasts, his rampant erection bumping into the dimpled V crowning the shadowy valley between Genetta's buttocks every time she ground her hips. His hands were still cupping her buttocks too, lifting her up and guiding her forward at the same time.

The master was guiding proceedings more and more insistently from behind, and his chest came increasingly into contact with Genetta's back as she moved. She leaned forward, which rotated her bottom away from the slave's mouth, but put her clit deliciously back into contact. The slave flicked it and rolled her tongue around it before suckling it into her mouth, like a luscious grape, and Genetta moaned as that hot streak of orgasm-chasing pain and pleasure raced through her again.

And then she felt it; she felt the helmet of the master's erection. 'Oh yes,' she sighed, arching her back and making herself completely available for him.

'You're too high,' he growled through gritted teeth. 'Get your arse down lower.'

A moment of doubt planted itself in Genetta's mind;

was this what she wanted? Did she really want a complete stranger to do this to her? But on the other hand it would almost certainly feel very, very good – as good as the slave sucking her pussy.

So she lowered her bottom, just as he demanded.

The insistent master pressed on her hip with one hand, Genetta let him manoeuvre her body to the angles he wanted, and he began stroking his cock against her.

The shaft of his penis slid up and down, investigating the smoothness of her snug, deep valley, and she moaned as the slave's mouth stopped pleasuring her. She bowed her body, tucking her stomach in, and looked down to see what was happening.

The master was fucking his slave's mouth. His erection was sinking down into her mouth, stretching her lips with its impressive girth, and she was sucking it with avid gusto. Genetta could hear the wet suckling sounds, which combined with the heady sight of the flushed face impaled by the gnarled column of rigid flesh, turned her on incredibly.

Then things got even more intense as Genetta watched the master pull the length of his penis out of his slave's mouth, and felt him pressing his insistent hardness against the tight entrance to her bottom, the plum-shaped head of his cock demanding entry into her private rear passage.

Genetta laid forward, her pussy still over the other slave's mouth, and gripped the edge of the platform that raised the three of them. She felt the slave's hair tickle her tummy, but that sensation was soon overwhelmed by what was happening to her from behind.

It seared – the master's cock pushing into her, taking what he wanted – seared and stretched and hurt.

'Relax,' he commanded gruffly, and she tried, but she

had never been over enamoured when Marie played with her anus, and she was not sure she liked what was happening now either. Especially with something so big and hard and demanding trying to gain entry.

'I'm not very far in,' he grunted dispassionately. 'Relax… relax and push back at me.'

Genetta squeezed her eyes shut and wished this was over. 'I – I'm not your slave,' she said through gritted teeth.

'You are my slave for the nonce,' he countered, and used his open palm to smack her rump. But he withdrew the few inches of his penis that had been inside her, and then pushed the heel of his hand down into the shapely dip of her back. For a fleeting second it crossed Genetta's mind that he was going to smother his slave, squashing her body over the woman's face like that, but the master did not seem worried. And Genetta had self-preservation on her mind, not concerns about someone else's comfort.

'I-I'm not sure I want to do this,' she blurted.

'But I'm afraid you have to,' he insisted. 'It is, after all, no more than you told us you wanted.'

'It looks wonderful,' encouraged the slave holding the mirror. 'I think you're going to love it.'

Genetta took a quick sidelong glance at him, and saw the reflection of the master kneeling behind her, his purplish shaft standing proud and ready. 'You really want to do this to me, don't you?' she said, and the master looked at the mirror and met her eyes there. He nodded, so Genetta closed her eyes and braced herself.

'Relax…' he coaxed again, but he did not wait any longer. His cock, hard as a mace, pressed into her again. Genetta dipped her back, her stomach flattened against the slave's face, and she cried out as the master sank all seven of his pulsing inches deep into her bowels.

He held still for long, long seconds, allowing Genetta a little moment to become somewhat accustomed to the feel of having her rectum invaded, and then he began to move.

Without consideration and without gentleness – just unyielding flesh ploughing in and out of her bottom. But then something gave inside her and the feelings changed. She was losing her bottom's virginity, it occurred to her, and then, when she grasped that thought and accepted it, having her bottom breached like her pussy felt incredibly good.

The master must have sensed that she was starting to enjoy herself, because after a few heavenly strokes he selfishly pulled out of her. '*Please...*' Genetta groaned desperately. 'I want more...'

'You'll get it when I feel like giving it to you,' he retorted. 'But for the time being...'

Genetta felt that familiar sliding within the divide of her bottom, and once again she peered through lust-filled eyes to see what was happening.

The slave lying beneath her was giving his erect cock full access to her mouth's pleasures again. Genetta blanched to think of sucking a hard-on that had just been in someone else's bottom, but the slave seemed to want it. She was making avaricious sounds in her throat and Genetta saw her hands petting and squeezing her master's thighs. Her fingers travelled behind his legs, up to his bottom, and he leaned into his slave's face some more. Genetta knew the slave was pushing her fingers into his anus, searching for his prostate.

He was deep in his slave's mouth, but that wasn't enough. Once again he pulled himself from her and poked at Genetta's backdoor. So she relaxed and let him in again, and when he was fully embedded, she turned to gaze in the mirror.

And the image that presented itself to her misty eyes was beautiful. His male form knelt possessively behind her, and beneath her, paying homage to her sensuality, was the curvaceous, milky-white perfection of the female slave. The master's head was bent forward and with staring eyes he was watching his length disappear into her tight bottom with every deep thrust. His slave's hands were working on his bottom and she was writhing – she could see where his cock was going and no doubt wished it were up inside her. Genetta looked at her own body. Her breasts were swaying and heaving, her rump was turned up, and she was straddling another woman's face, a woman who was waiting her turn to serve a master's needs with her servile lips and tongue.

This… this, at last, was Genetta's idea of submission.

Chapter Nine

Genetta twirled around the living room, trailing two dresses on hangers on either side of her.

'I'm going back to the club,' she said to herself, in between the bars of a little song she made up as she went. 'And I'm going to be the belle of the ball.'

Stopping in front of the window she held one dress out and appraised it, and her ghostly reflection in the glass modelled the dress held in front of her at arm's length. She looked at it with a sceptical eye, and then with a quick and flippant toss, landed the dress in a flimsy heap on one of the nearby chairs.

Her quick movement was mirrored once again by the curtain in the flat across the street. For a second Genetta's impulse was to jump and hide from her own uncovered window, just as she had done before. But as the curtain opposite moved aside again, slowly, she felt brazen. She felt mischievous, and she felt devilish.

She lowered her chin and stared under the fringe of her hair at the other window. Somebody over there was eager to see more. She had rather disappointed him the last time – assuming it *was* a him. Genetta glanced down at her almost naked body, wearing only her sexy little bra and knickers. Slowly, she began to twist her body back and forth at the waist, coquettishly, with her feet slightly parted. Her arms hung loose, and tantalisingly slowly, she placed a finger just above her navel. Still turning her torso from side to side, twisting at the waist, she slid her hand down towards her panties and pushed the extended finger under the elastic waistband.

The curtain opened a little more.

With agonising slowness, Genetta withdrew her fingertip from her burgundy silk panties and began back up the short journey to her navel. And she did not stop there. Tracing an invisible line up the centre of her stomach, she teased her fingertip up over the delicious curve of the underside of her matching bra cup.

Then she stood still, too. With her fingernail, she made a circle around her nipple, teasing it to fullness through the lacy material. The tickling sensation rocketed the nerves between her legs, making her hips gyrate fractionally.

She lifted her finger to her lips and licked it broadly before pushing it into her mouth. Her other fingers fanned before her eyes. She was peeking at the spy across from her, just as he hid and watched her.

Genetta sucked her finger, pushing it in and out of her mouth. Her hips still circled. She moved her other hand down the curve of her side, petting herself in a long stroke. When her palm was fully on her silk-clad hip, she walked her fingers across her lower stomach and slipped them down between her thighs.

She felt the steaminess through the crotch of her pants. Her cleft was wet.

But just as she prepared to push her fingers hard against her aching mound, the light across the way came on and she could see bustling movement behind the ivory chintz curtain.

Feeling strangely let down, she realised her voyeur was not going to stay around and watch the culmination of the show. Or more likely, he had been disturbed and *could* not stay around to watch. But with her one fingertip resting on her lower lip, her other hand lingering in front of her covered pussy, she watched her audience member's vantage point for another moment.

A black cab slid into her view in the street outside and settled itself in front of her window, between Genetta and her anonymous admirer. Its arrival reminded her that she had better get ready and head out to meet Tracey and Paul – her favourite new playmates – for a night of very public dancing, not just showing off for a voyeur.

With a sigh, she bent and grabbed the crumpled black heap of a dress from the chair. Turning it about quickly in order to find its hem, she dropped it over her head and shimmied into its tight fit. The cut and material moulded to her figure, leaving no secrets about her soft girlish shape.

Running back to her bedroom, she threw open the closet and found a pair of oh-so-sexy black stiletto spikes. 'Mankillers,' she said, smiling to herself, as she dropped them to the floor and stepped into them.

The heels lifted her a few inches, pushing her weight forward onto the balls of her feet. Genetta bent down and with guilty pleasure, ran her hands up her well-defined, bare calves. The muscles and tendons were flexed and sexy.

A knock sounded at the door, and furrowing her brow, she glanced at the bedside clock. True, she was cutting it a bit fine, but she had told Tracey that she'd go over to the flat her friend now shared with Paul, rather than they should come over to hers, because a trip to Genetta's meant backtracking for all of them to go to the best clubs.

'Just coming Trace!' she called, and walked quickly to the front door. The clicks of her high-heeled shoes alternated with the padding sound of their leather soles on the ceramic tile in the short hallway.

'I was just getting ready to come get you lot—' she announced as she undid the bolt and pulled the door open, but the force of the tackle knocked the breath from her lungs and her back into the room.

She gasped, winded, struggling to suck in air, and so swift and unexpected was the assault that she was unable to scream or cry for help.

The flat spun backwards over her head, the ceiling's length sweeping by quickly. The first man through the door, the one who had slammed into her midriff with the considerable weight of his body, grappled her down. She shut her eyes tight in a split second, expecting her head to smash onto the tiles, but a gloved hand cushioned what would have been a grimacing impact.

They lay there for a moment, the stranger on top of Genetta, she laying beneath his immense weight in stunned silence. She was still unable to react to the shock of what was happening to her.

What was happening to her?

The slam of the front door shutting brought her to her senses.

'Son of a bitch!' she shouted. Her legs and bare feet kicked as she tried to dislodge the bulky stranger. But he had, quite literally, knocked her out of her shoes and her heels drummed ineffectually against the backs of his thighs. 'W-who are you?' she shrieked. 'What – what the fuck do you think you're doing?!'

Struggling desperately, she managed to get one arm loose from under the elbow that attempted to clasp her, and quickly tried to drag the frightening black balaclava off her adversary's head. But he easily grabbed her wrist and pinned her arm back to the floor.

'C'mon, get her in here,' a man's voice barked, but the body on top of her only grunted in response.

She saw black polished combat boots with black twill trousers tucked into them as the second man walked by her. Genetta screamed, but the man on top of her yanked his other hand from under her head and clamped it aggressively over her open mouth. She bit into him as hard as she could, but to no avail because the thick leather of his gloves prevented her hurting him. He held her face tightly, squeezing her jaw between his fingers and the heel of his hand. Then menacingly, slowly, he lowered his head until his covered mouth rested right beside her ear.

'You're a much nicer girlie when you're wearing a butt plug,' he whispered hoarsely.

He raised his head and she looked long and hard into his calculating blue eyes. They were piercing, with a clear, knowing intelligence that returned her stare, and went further; deep into her heart.

'I-I don't know you,' she countered timidly.

'But Genetta, I know you.'

'It doesn't matter either way,' the other intruder interrupted. 'It doesn't matter one little bit. Are you going to do what we said?' he went on, looking to his formidable associate.

Genetta's eyes flickered slightly from the sound of that oddly familiar voice, to the gaze that formed the threatening blue of a hot flame right over her face. Her lips formed to ask the question that hung in the air – she was helpless to do anything else.

'Wha-what are you going to do to me?' she stumbled, not really sure she wanted to hear the response.

'Don't worry,' her captor said. 'We're not going to

hurt you, if that's what you're thinking.'

'I wouldn't go that far,' his accomplice sniggered from somewhere beyond Genetta's restricted field of vision. 'We might hurt you a little. But only for fun... just for fun.'

She clamped her eyes tight shut. She had to collect her thoughts and some semblance of composure. She had to think straight if she was to get out of this bizarre predicament unscathed.

But her spinning mind could not override her body's impulse to resist this totally bewildering outrage. Her adrenalin was pumping and her body wanted to fight, and she instinctively twisted her torso and shoulders violently and as quickly as she could.

'That's enough!' the man on top of her hissed, pinning her down without too much difficulty.

'Let me deal with her,' the other man said, and again she almost managed to place his voice. But her attempts at recollection were scattered when he knelt by her head, gripped her wrists painfully, and hauled them back, pressing them together on the floor above her head. She cried out again, but her strained cursing turned to silence, her throat was so tight with fear. He also wore a foreboding black balaclava.

'Genetta, you have to calm down,' the man on top of her said, and then with a leather thumb he traced her cheekbone back into her hairline. 'No one's here to hurt you. We just want to give you pleasure. Now, doesn't that sound nice?'

'I – I don't know,' she managed. 'I don't understand what you mean. What kind of a game is this?'

'Play along with the fact that I'm the considerate one – the easygoing one,' he told her. 'He's the heavy. But neither of us is going to cause you harm. All right? I want to make your fantasies come true, baby. That's all.'

She closed her eyes, willing herself to understand what he meant.

The man on top of her shifted his hips and her legs opened around him. She felt him give a gentle push against her. She gasped; his cock was so hard, and as he began circling his hips, moving his stiffness against her crotch, she felt her shameful body respond to the slow, rhythmic dance.

'I do want some pleasure,' she murmured, her eyes still closed.

'And you need a lot of it, don't you?' he said softly. 'That's why there are two of us here. We want to take turns with you. We can service your body's needs all night, if you can keep up with us.'

'Yes,' she whispered, opening her eyes to look into his once more. 'I do want it.'

'We know you do.'

'I want you both… all night.'

'Good girl,' he whispered emphatically. 'I'm going to put a blindfold on you now, all right? We don't want you seeing us, but we do want to take off these hot clothes so we can be more intimate with you.'

'All right,' she said, and suddenly her thoughts cleared and she heard the accent she'd not heard before because of the shock and pandemonium of the assault. She heard the accent and she recognised the other's voice too: They were Jack Adams and Paul!

The one leaning on her arms, Jack, produced a black silk scarf from a pocket. 'I'm going to release your arms now, Gen,' he said. 'But you be a good girl for me, and don't move.'

'Yes, sir,' she said, and began to relax a little in the knowledge that she knew them and she was not in any danger.

'Oh, what a lovely response,' Paul said. The lump in his trousers was still grinding against her, keeping her afloat on a sea of desire. 'How deliciously respectful.'

Genetta opened her eyes to see him glance at Jack. 'Go ahead, she's ready,' he said, then looked back down at her. 'And while he does that, I'm going to do this…' He lifted himself until he was kneeling between her sprawled legs. Spellbound, Genetta watched him unbutton his trousers before the soft blindfold fell across her eyes and caressed the bridge of her nose.

Lifting her head allowed Jack to tie it tightly, knotting it in her soft hair. 'I've tied the knot at the side so you can rest your head comfortably,' he said. 'All right?'

'Thank you…' she said, just before she felt a finger insinuate itself under the crotch of her panties and into her sex. 'Oh,' she groaned, and arched her back.

'She's quite ready,' Paul said, moving his finger up and down, sliding it against her wet path. 'All right then, sweetheart,' he went on, 'you can call him One and me Two, but I don't expect it'll make much difference to you in a little while who's called what. Okay then, let's have you up, shall we?'

For a brief moment Genetta felt their separate presences disappear and leave her alone, then someone took her hand and lifted her to her feet. Her skirt slipped down around her upper thighs as she stood, then a pair of hands reached up under it and made her move to the side and take a step back. Her other foot followed and instinctively she clasped her thighs together.

'None of that,' Paul said, and she knew he was the one

messing about with her. So she obediently relaxed, and he tugged her panties down over her smooth, slightly parted thighs. As they passed her knees she lifted one foot, he drew the panties over it, and then she lifted the other as he waited.

'Here, baby,' he went on, encouraging her, and she felt the delicate silk of her own panties against her lips.

'No,' she protested, moving her face to the side a little, but as she opened her mouth to utter the denial he pushed the tiny perfumed bundle between her lips and held them there. She lifted her hands to his wrists and pushed a little so he would remove the panties and she could speak. 'Please stop it, sir, I don't want—'

'To be utterly helpless?' Jack asked from somewhere nearby. 'I thought that was the whole point, Genetta – for you to feel utterly helpless and out of control. To put your fate in someone else's hands.' His voice came closer as he spoke.

She turned towards him, blind beneath the silk scarf around her head.

'Jack?'

'Why would you call me that?' One replied.

Before she could answer she sighed and inhaled deeply as someone began kneading her breasts with both hands. 'I-I don't know,' she stammered quietly. 'What you just said…' Her voice was trembling and she found it difficult to talk or even think from traces of fear, confusion and ever-increasing desire.

One helped her. 'What did I just say, my dear girl?'

'You said something that… that I never told anyone… anyone but Jack – Jack Adams.'

'And what did you tell him, exactly?'

'I told him about losing control,' she answered openly.

'About my fantasy for being taken away and used.'

'Perhaps you told Jack those things, and now you've told Two, and me. More and more people are learning about your fantasies. And as I said, we want to make them come true for you. Be calm, my dear girl, and no harm will come to you.'

Genetta moaned softly as his fingertips captured her nipples and squeezed them. He rolled them gently and she pushed her hips forward, towards him.

'That's my girl,' he whispered, and put a finger under her chin. 'Tilt your head back and open your mouth.'

She complied, and the warm silk of her panties again pressed between her lips and onto her tongue. She opened her jaw wider still, and tasted their damp muskiness as they filled her mouth.

'Come on, now,' One said, and for a fleeting moment she wondered why they had brought anonymity into the game. And how they had gotten together to give her this experience was also a mystery, but she had no time to think about it further. One took her upper arm and turned her gently. Genetta followed his lead.

She stopped when her thighs nudged the arm of the settee.

'If you keep being such a good girl, we won't bind you,' Jack stated. 'Understand?'

Genetta nodded.

'Good,' Paul said, his satisfaction evident in his tone, and then he touched her shoulder and pressed her forward.

She bent her knees and braced them against the side of the sofa before extending her arms and lowering herself forward. The cushion on the couch met her cheek, and she was bent completely from the waist. For comfort's sake, to ease the strain on her hamstrings and calves, she extended her legs behind her until she was resting on her toes, and slid her tummy forward a little until the arm of the settee was right under her hips, bracing and presenting her for the delectation of the men who waited patiently.

Clothes began dropping to the floor – she could hear them. She imagined that the two of them started with their gloves, then the balaclavas, taking off those hot covers so they could be more comfortable. Then she heard the sound of a belt being unbuckled, then a zip and the sounds of trousers sliding down legs.

What would they want from her first?

'I need to fuck her,' Paul said frankly.

'Go ahead,' Jack acquiesced. 'There's plenty more for me to enjoy.'

Paul positioned himself behind her, moving her hips to suit his needs. She lifted her bottom a little when she felt the head of his penis butt against her pussy, nestling in her soft curly pubic hair.

With a push forward the head of his cock made its way almost into her. She was not wet enough, she sensed, but with another shunt his erection sank into her. Genetta moaned, the sound muted by her silky gag.

He forged into her, and the sudden pressure of his groin against her taut buttocks drove her down and forward into the cushions and against the arm of the settee, sandwiching her there.

But the delicious fullness inside her sex more than made up for any discomfort. Paul was deep in her body, and it felt as if he were bracing his feet against the floor so he could drive in even harder.

Genetta lifted her face, strained her neck to hold her head higher, and her back arched as Paul grabbed her hips, squeezed them and began pumping feverishly.

As much as she could, Genetta ground back against him. She tried to match his every stroke with a turning up of her bottom so he could sink his erection deeper and deeper.

'Oh, you're gorgeous,' he panted in her ear, and she knew that the sight of her slave's face, adorned with the blindfold, her moist lips slightly parted and her white panties showing between them, inspired him as he started driving in and out like a piston.

She was wet, and Paul's rigid cock made juicy succulent sounds every time he pounded into her to the hilt.

Then a similar but softer sound interrupted her bliss. She tuned into it, listening more carefully, and realised that Jack was kneeling on the edge of the settee and was masturbating right next to her face. His fingers probed between her lips and tugged on the panties, pulling them free, and then his cock was fed into her mouth in their place.

Genetta opened for him and felt his unyielding flesh press deep, nudging the back of her throat. Her nose was buried for a moment in his pubic hair, and then he pulled back from her. Genetta tightened her lips and felt each throbbing vein slide against them as he drew his staff out. The ridge under his glans rested just inside her lips, the head of his rod keeping them stretched, before he pushed once again towards her throat.

Now she had one rutting at her from behind and one easing his cock in and out of her face. She tilted her head up a little more to let Jack enjoy the sight of his shaft riding in and out of her mouth. Obviously, Paul was watching as well – and was increasingly aroused by what he saw. His thrusts plunged into her with ever-increasing ferocity. His balls were swinging and slapping between the very tops of her tensed thighs, and she could hear the sound of his groin smacking her buttocks every time he plunged into her.

And with increasing intensity Jack was giving her the same treatment. He took two handfuls of her hair and held her head in place. Genetta complied; trying to hold still despite the pounding she was receiving at her rear.

'Play with yourself,' one of the men grunted – in her delirium she wasn't sure which. But she obediently pressed a hand between her stomach and the sofa, difficult as it was with the arm of it pressing into her midriff, and inched her fingers towards her aching clit. When her fingertips reached the hot button she circled it briefly, teasing herself. Then she continued her movement across her pussy, until her index and middle fingers formed a V around Paul's plunging, slippery length.

Genetta squeezed her fingers together gently and he groaned. 'That's it, baby, show me you want it,' he gasped, and she pushed the tips of her fingers into her well, next to his delving pole.

'Take my cock,' Jack said, and twisting slightly from the waist she rested her shoulder on the sofa and lifted her other hand. He pulled out of her mouth, she fumbled blindly to grasp his pulsing cock, and he helped, guiding her hand and wrapping her fingers around its powerful length. Genetta began stroking him.

'I'm going to come on your face now,' Jack told her, his voice strained.

Something brushed against her cheek, and Genetta turned her face towards the feeling. It was her silken panties; Jack was rubbing them on her skin as she masturbated him. She licked her lips and moved her mouth towards the underwear, and when her lips were touching them, she nipped some of the material between her teeth and held them there.

'That's it,' Jack encouraged. 'Make me come now.'

Obediently, Genetta maintained the pace as she slid her fist up and down his shaft, the collar of skin moving back and forth. Paul, in the meantime, had slowed his frantic thrusting and was easing his erection back and forth in her body. Genetta's breasts were pressing against Jack's knees, and she knew his penis was threatening to erupt at any moment.

'Oh yeah, I'm going to come all over your gorgeous face,' Jack repeated.

Paul groaned behind her and gave her a good hard thrust. He kept his erection buried in her and began grinding in a tight circle. Genetta pressed her bottom back at him, reciprocating every movement.

'I'm going to come now too,' he rasped breathlessly, and as he shunted against her bottom she nudged forward and Jack's cock squeezed against her cheek, and that was all the extra stimulation he needed.

The first eruption coated her lower lip and immediately dribbled down her chin. She opened her mouth wider to take the next shot, and as Jack clamped his hand over hers she squeezed her fist up his staff, bringing the next ejaculation with it.

It landed on her blindfold and cheek and she felt it sliding down to the corner of her gasping mouth. Jack ran his thumb and fingers over her hot face, smearing his come into her flushed complexion. At the same moment Paul braced his knees between hers, pinned her midriff heavily to the settee, and grunted like an animal. She felt his thigh muscles tense, felt his fingers tighten around her trim waist, and she felt him coming deep within her...

'Thank you,' Genetta whispered breathlessly to both men when Paul eventually withdrew and their urgency had eased a little.

'She's great,' Paul said. 'She is great,' he repeated, emphasising the compliment by stating each word slowly.

'She is a very good girl,' Jack concurred. His fingers were still straying idly over her face as she rested on the sofa.

'I think she's ready,' Paul said, as his hands ran over the tensed muscles in her back, down over her lovely buttocks and down to the backs of her toned thighs. With what felt like a protective gesture, he pulled the hem of her dress down to cover her.

'Here, let her put her panties back on,' Jack said, passing them to Paul, who bent down and helped her step into them, one foot at a time.

'And her shoes,' Jack directed, clearly in charge.

Paul collected them and again helped her, assisting her to stand and bending to guide her feet into the shoes.

'Is the cab still out there?' he asked.

'It better be.' Jack was putting on his clothes, Genetta could tell from the sounds. She heard him walk across the room to the window overlooking the street. 'Yeah, it's still there,' he confirmed.

'Okay, let's go,' Paul said.

Crossing her arms over her breasts, Genetta held the lapels of her coat; draped around her shoulders by one of the men.

Without removing the blindfold, the men escorted her to the front door. When it shut behind her, Genetta listened to the echo in the small hallway and knew that once again, she was leaving the life she had known behind.

Chapter Ten

The blindfold sat snug against the bridge of her nose. It tucked in under her eyes and rested on her cheekbones. No light penetrated it. Genetta could see nothing.

One of the men held her elbow firmly and walked just behind her. Instinctively, finding the concept of having no sight disturbingly alarming, she reached out and found the back and shoulder of the guardian in front. She let her fingers brush him lightly, the men's steady walking set the pace and Genetta could do nothing but keep time and trust that they would not let her fall.

When the cool night air caressed her face, she knew they had left her building. The city air could not seem to clear itself of the biting smell of fumes from buses and cars, not even this late in the evening. The cab door opened and the first man got in, then the one behind her pushing down on the back of her head. She ducked and bent at the waist and into the London cab she climbed. The bench seat to her right was easy to find as she stumbled a little inside the cab's roomy interior. A strong hand on one side of her bottom pressed her hips around and she lowered herself onto the slightly squeaky seat.

Inside the chugging vehicle it was close. Genetta was hot within the coat her captors had put on her. It lay heavily on her shoulders. The cab smelt of ammonia and disinfectant – astringent, but with an earthy smell emanating like a low note. It was the scent left by countless bodies pressing into the vinyl seats. Sweat and skin and clothing, breath and hair and perfumes and colognes mingling with tobacco and liquor. The odours commingled to leave an overall impression of the essence of a typical London fare, and Genetta could not help but think that a blindfolded submissive could not be a particularly typical London fare. She could not help but wonder what the cabdriver must think of such strange passengers, but quickly concluded that he must be on their payroll, if only for the relatively short time he was of use to them.

The cab moved off, but she had not heard either of her keepers give a destination. Try as she might to suppress any anxiety, Genetta was getting nervy again. In the flat Jack and Paul had her devoted attention; lust had stopped her thinking constructively. But now, with nothing to do but question her fate, Genetta wanted some answers.

'Would someone please tell me what's going on?' she asked gingerly.

'You'll figure it out soon enough,' Paul replied.

'And what happens if I don't want to play this game any more?' she pressed.

Jack chuckled. 'Now I have a question,' he said testily. 'When the hell are you going to understand that you're nothing more than our slave? You don't seem to ever learn that your opinions and wants are fast becoming of little consequence.'

'She keeps trading hands,' Paul continued in the same vein. 'But no, she never gets it that she doesn't find a good trainer because she's a bad slave. And she's a bad slave because she hasn't accepted that she no longer has her own will. She must see it as constant manipulation or we're fooling her or something. She doesn't seem to notice the design. Genetta has to learn that her only value lies in how well she serves our requirements – and that's it.'

'A bad slave,' Jack said in a tone of agreement. Then both men were quiet and Genetta was left to sit and contemplate their brutal words.

Being called a bad slave did not sit well with her. 'Does a bad slave enjoy her subservience?' she challenged meekly. 'Well, I can do that. I really loved being submissive to the two of you back there, so surely I must be a good slave.'

'No, Genny, you're rather missing the point once again,' Paul said arrogantly. 'A good slave doesn't necessarily like or enjoy her status.'

'A good slave has no opinion at all about her status,' Jack continued. 'It's not something that gives her constant enjoyment and pleasure. She does not always have things to suit her. A good slave's submission goes beyond the separate sexual incidents that fill her nights. A proper, well-behaved submissive's entire life is spent in an attitude of quiet, unperturbed waiting for a chance to be of service.'

Genetta thought for a few moments, alone as she was behind the darkness of the blindfold. The cab made its way through London's streets and she sensed briefly that the driver did not seem to hurry through the traffic. The way forward was smooth and steady.

'Will I have an opportunity to serve you some more?' she asked in a quiet, respectful voice.

'You will serve us by quite simply doing as you are told,' Jack told her. 'It's as easy as that, Genetta. You need not struggle with your subservience or the way you've been treated or over what the future holds. All you have to concern yourself with from now on is listening and performing the tasks given to you. You must stop having opinions about your position and place. Do you understand?'

She nodded in response, but her heart was not so positive about it. If she understood what Jack was saying, she did not like his idea of silent submission at all.

The threesome continued their London journey in a seemingly companionable quiet. There was no sense of anticipation that Genetta could feel emanating from the men on either side of her. The emotional atmosphere in the cab was sombre, as if there were a serious task that needed seeing to.

The car pulled over to the kerb and Jack opened the door. Genetta extended her hand, he took it, and she stepped carefully to the pavement. Behind her, she heard Paul talking to the driver in a low but hurried tone.

'Something new, Genny,' Jack said as he took her elbow and walked her briskly along. 'A chance to show me that you comprehend the placid, giving attitude I want you to adopt.'

'Where's Paul?' she asked.

'Paul's gone back to his little lady; we doubt very much that she'd have approved of our little game this evening.'

They stopped suddenly. 'Revolving door,' Jack said, letting go of her arm. 'Step into it, and keep walking until I catch you on the other side. Now—' he gave her a push and Genetta caught her stride as the spinning door gave her another shove from behind.

'Right, now this way,' Jack said in her ear, once they were both clear of the door. His softened American accent still had that note of competent command that had attracted her to him in the first place.

In the first place…

Had everything always been interrelated? Had every step of her life led her inexorably toward this moment? Jack,

Marie, Tracey and Paul – had everyone always been involved in leading her to servitude?

If there were such a thing as fate, Genetta pondered, then maybe this was hers. Maybe she was beginning to see what Jack and Paul meant. Maybe there was no agreeing or disagreeing with her slavery. Perhaps she could not go to the club and pursue a master, nor could she avoid being taken by one. She was a submissive and that was her only role.

Jack stopped and she heard a door open in front of her. Without stepping into the room, she could hear the rapid click-clack sound of a film projector's turning reels, and when Jack took her hand and pulled her through the doorway, Genetta was nearly overcome by heart-quickening apprehension.

'I don't want to,' she whispered, as the close, cigar-laden atmosphere hit her. 'There's something… no Jack, please, let's leave.'

'Remember what we explained to you on our way over here,' he responded, closing the door behind them.

'No, there's something…' she repeated, 'something not right.'

'It's just a few of my closest acquaintances, my dear,' he explained, whispering slightly, not wanting to disturb the others in the room. 'This is a private club and cinema we own, and where we come to get away from the stresses of the outside world. We relax over a drink and a cigar, chat about business, and watch films.

'This film, for example,' he went on, 'is about a delicious new submissive who allows men to use her for their pleasure. She asks no questions, makes no fuss. She just lies on a sofa, looking very pretty in her black hood, and lets the punters enjoy her.'

Genetta's throat was so dry and tight she could barely manage a whisper. 'Where was it shot?' she asked – but she already knew where.

'Oh, some place familiar to you,' he said, confirming her worst fears. 'Familiar to you now, that is. It wasn't then.'

Genetta's chest tightened and she felt dizzy. She could not breathe or move. 'My – my address book, Jack,' she said weakly, pieces beginning to drop into place. 'What did you do with it?'

'It's in safekeeping, Gen, you're not to worry,' he said warmly, but she did worry. 'It's with a few copies of this film.'

'What do you mean to do with all of it?'

'I mean to retain it for safekeeping, as I said. But do not worry; I doubt if even your family or friends could recognise you in the condition you were that night.'

'Stop it,' she said.

'But you haven't done anything to stop yet,' he said in such a smarmy tone that Genetta knew he was enjoying himself immensely. She did not need to see his face to know that.

'Was it all planned?' she asked, because she had to know. 'From the beginning?'

'Yours is not to reason why,' Jack answered, and they began moving again. 'Or to reason how. Yours is just to perform well for my friends.'

When her knee nudged something hard, she stopped. Jack seemed to be off to the side. He took her shoulders and turned her. Then he pushed gently against the middle of her back and Genetta took a step sideways.

As the backs of her legs brushed against something Genetta felt sick again, but even more nauseous than she'd felt when Jack had let on that he could send a copy of her shameful performance to her family and friends. All of them, all of the people whom she'd trusted or liked or been attracted to or friends with – they had all used her and apparently sold the evidence of her vulnerability for distribution. She was nothing to these people – but they had been something to her.

A pair of hands grabbed her shoulders and pushed her further to the side. Then another pair of hands grabbed her hips and pulled her down.

Genetta really did not want to sit on anyone's lap, but if that was Jack pushing her down – and it was, she could sense it – then she had to do his bidding. She had to be the good slave; she had to be the grateful stolen servant.

The seated man moved his knees and they bumped against the backs of her thighs. His hands left her hips and he tugged up the back of her leather coat, lifted the skirt of her dress, and peeled her panties down to her knees, where they hovered for a second, and then shimmied smoothly down to her ankles. When she felt the warm air against her bottom, she allowed Jack's hands to lower her to the stranger's lap, knowing it was expected of her.

With the man's hands clasping her hips again, he quickly manoeuvred her as he wanted. Genetta lifted a hand to her shoulder, to where Jack's lay, and warmth comforted her as she felt him squeeze her fingers; he was there for her. He would witness this, and know that she was doing it all for him – he would know that she was trying to be the good slave, for him.

The sitting man's cock pressed upwards. His movements felt urgent, barely controlled. Genetta compliantly allowed him to position her, and then with a sudden and aggressive thrust of his hips he impaled her.

Her weight was on his lap and his vertical column of flesh was buried high up inside her, making her inhale deeply and then hold her breath, while he grunted as she instinctively slid up and down on him.

Getting it from behind like this reminded her of how Jack had bound, gagged and used her that first night. Was that his intention? Did he want her to remember that night and to feel his mastery over her even now, as another man's cock filled her sex?

Jack's hand was still with hers. Genetta bobbed up and down, a good slave, using her velvety pussy to milk the hard cock inside her.

Perspiration meandered between her breasts and down her back, and she heard more men stirring and murmuring.

The sight of her, blindfolded, leather coat gaping to show off her cleavage, squirming up and down on the man sitting beneath her – all captured in the silvery, fragmenting glow from the screen must have been extremely erotic. Genetta wished someone would speak, would compliment her directly on appearance or performance… but she pushed that thought aside.

She was serving Jack. Letting these men fuck her was a service to her master.

The man beneath her came. She felt his thighs tense, his hands clamp her waist even tighter, and heard him inhale sharply.

He pushed her up and away as soon as she was finished. Genetta took an unsteady few steps, losing her panties as she did, and then another man pulled her down. 'My turn to fuck you now,' a low, threatening voice whispered.

In response, Genetta writhed against him. They moved until he had his erection partly inside her, then he gave an abrupt shove that made her squeal and took her breath away, and penetrated her fully.

When again used to the sensation of being completely filled, she held him inside her depths and began rocking. Back and forth she rode, giving him a tantalising amount of friction, and he did not last long. As his back straightened, shoulders against his chair, and he lifted her up with his hips, Genetta again reached out blindly for Jack. And he was still there.

She was passed to a third man, all the while holding Jack's hands. She pushed her bottom back, he too held her hips in place right over the head of his shaft, and then drove up into her.

Jack pulled his fingers from their entwining with hers and Genetta felt him take hold of her wrists. Then he caressed his way up her forearms to her biceps, and then his fingertips brushed her breasts.

He took his hands away and she heard the sound of leather slipping through belt loops, just like before when she had been with him.

He dropped the belt across her wrists and his hands went straight back up to her breasts. Roughly, he pinched her nipples.

Genetta let out another little squeal and Jack twisted each nipple between thumb and finger – the feeling so particular she knew precisely what he was doing to her.

The man beneath her was grinding his hips up against her bottom as Jack stretched his fingers out to encompass each breast. As the man screwing her went deep into her body, then pulled out just a fraction before driving in again, Jack was squeezing her breasts harder and harder. His grip was vicelike and he crushed her breasts as if he meant to hurt her.

The pain began to evaporate Genetta's consciousness. It swelled up beneath all the other feelings and thoughts that she could have been experiencing, and it subsumed everything into itself. Like a kraken rising from the deep, mouth gaping, it sucked in her identity and reduced her body to a servant to feed its titan appetite for pain.

And still Jack tortured her breasts. And still the man pushed up into her. Genetta let her head drop back and clenched her teeth. She would bear this, no matter what. Taking this meant she was a good slave, and she would prove that she could be one.

She did not know when Jack let go of her breasts. The pain had an echo that continued even after the immediate pressure was gone. She only noticed the greater change when she felt him putting the belt around her ribs. When he was holding it tightly around her chest, his hard knuckles pushing against her, he pulled her up and with a shove, sent her stumbling on to the next man.

The leather strap was cutting into the soft flesh of her breasts as she slumped onto the next man's lap. He pushed the head of his phallus against her rear. She slid forward a little to give him better access, pushed back against him and winced as his glans pushed into her anus. At the same time Jack was tightening the belt with purposeful jerks.

The other man was filling her bottom, pulling her down and back, forcing her to take it up her behind, while Jack kept tightening the belt.

Leverage was working for him. Jack pulled the loose end of the strap to the side, sliding it back along the buckle that held it in place. All the while it was constricting her breasts, crushing her nipples beneath it.

When the belt was as tight as it could possibly be, Jack gave it one more tug, then fastened it. Genetta was finding it difficult to concentrate on the penis inside her, and the man sitting beneath her was getting frustrated. He slapped her hip, and she knew it was a reminder of what she should be doing – providing him with pleasure – but she heard Jack reprimand the man for striking her.

So he was acting as her master. He was protecting her from harm, even while he put her in a position to degrade her and show her that she was a toy to him – and to anyone with whom he cared to share her body's pleasures.

Genetta backed herself down hard onto the man's lap. When she had him in to the hilt, she started rocking back and forth, holding him in as deep as she could. His thighs were tight together and she was straddling his legs.

The unknown man shuddered and she heard him groan, 'Yes, that's it… *yes*.'

Genetta was physically drained, but felt she understood her purpose now. It was to serve Jack by being a sponge for the punishment he wanted to give her. She must learn to find her satisfaction within that role.

'Are you ready to do more of what I tell you?' Jack asked.

'I – yes, I think so,' she answered tentatively. 'I want to please you, Jack.'

'Good, because you've some more work to do.'

The cold air hit her face again and she knew they were outside. Her sense of direction was greatly turned about, but she thought they were heading back to the cab. When she heard its chugging diesel engine and the rear door open, she knew she was right.

'Get in,' Jack said brusquely. She reached out and felt for the opening, then leaned in and found the seat with her hand before raising herself into the cab.

She sat down, and then realised that Jack had not

followed her, that he was still standing outside with the door open.

'Okay,' he said, 'the driver knows where to take you.'

'By myself?' Genetta gasped, suddenly feeling empty and very alone.

'Yes, by yourself,' he confirmed. 'You don't need me to help you with this part.'

He slammed the door shut and with Genetta blindfolded and sitting alone in the back, the cab moved off.

Chapter Eleven

Genetta put her head against the window and took a deep breath. She did not think of any questions or utter a sound as the cab pulled away from the kerb.

As the car drove down city streets, she slowly gathered more control of herself. Touching her face, she found the edge of the blindfold. She tugged it down below her chin and blinked out at the night from the back of the cab.

The driver was careful, not jolting her, so she sat back in the seat and relaxed some. It did not seem to matter to him if she took off the blindfold or not – he did not appear to be paying any attention to her – so she reached behind her neck and began pulling at the knot there.

When it came free, she pulled the scarf off and shook her hair free of it. When she thought of how she had been used she started to tremble a little, and actually began to feel a little nauseous again. Never before had she felt so utterly used. But she had accepted it all at Jack's behest, so it served some purpose… perhaps.

A sob caught in her throat. How had she reached such a point? How had she allowed all this to happen to her?

She leant forward to tap on the screen dividing her from the cabdriver.

'Take me home,' she said, raising her voice to be heard through the glass partition, trying to get a better look at him.

'Hey…' she said, louder still. 'Didn't you hear me? I

said I want to go home.'

'Right,' he at last acknowledged her, shrugging his shoulders without taking his eyes from the road.

But they were heading in a direction Genetta did not recognise, so she thumped the glass divider with her palm. 'Excuse me, but I said—'

'I heard what you said,' he snarled, his instant aggression making her flinch back a little and snuffing the words out at the back of her throat. 'And do that again and you're on your own out on the pavement. D'you hear?'

'I'm sorry,' Genetta blurted hastily. 'I didn't mean anything by it... but where are we going?'

He reached back to the window at an awkward angle and dragged it open. 'Nothing outside looks familiar to you, eh?' he asked, his flash temper apparently appeased for the moment.

Feeling utterly exhausted and highly confused, Genetta sat back resignedly and looked out at the passing streets beneath the glow of the orange streetlights. 'No,' she said finally, 'nothing at all.'

'Odd that,' he muttered, then said, 'Look, you let me know if you figure out your whereabouts before we reach the destination your friends had in mind, yeah?'

And so a silence fell between the two of them, but gradually Genetta began to see landmarks – streets and stores – that looked more and more familiar.

And then it dawned on her.

Marie! Jack was sending her back to Marie! He was sending her back to her onetime mistress – to the house where Genetta had served.

'Good God,' she said softly. 'I'm going back to where it all started; to the person who started it. Back to the beginning that leads to... here and now.'

The driver took the cab around a few corners, meandering down residential Notting Hill streets at a crawl.

'I know where we are,' Genetta told him quietly.

'Good – makes it easier if you tell me when we pass the right door.'

'Okay, stop here,' she instructed him. 'I can walk the rest.'

'Sorry love, your friends were quiet clear – door-to-door service is required. You're very precious cargo, apparently, and they've paid me well to make sure you get to where you're going safely.'

'So you're not actually involved in any of this.'

'Nope. I'm just the man driving the cab, that's all. Once I've delivered you, you'll never see me again.'

'All of this is going on around you and your taxi and you don't belong to the club? You're not in the scene?'

He shook his head, his eyes scanning the door numbers as they passed. 'I ain't got a clue what you're on about. Ain't got a clue about clubs and scenes. I just drive and deliver – and keep myself to myself.'

'I don't believe it.'

'You don't have to. As I say, I was well paid tonight right from the outset. I just radioed the base, said I was engaged all evening and would have the cash to show for it later. Only stipulation on this side was that I keep shtum about everything I see and hear during the job.'

'And you think you can?' Genetta asked, also looking out for the door she would recognise as Marie's.

'Blimey, love,' he chuckled, 'who would believe such a tale as I've seen tonight?

'Besides…' he added thoughtfully, and in the gloom of the cab Genetta sensed a worrying change in his demeanour.

'Besides, what?' she asked a little anxiously, as he looked over his should to park the cab in a tight spot between two cars beside the kerb.

Once skilfully and easily parked the cabbie turned around fully and looked at her with a deep frown. Then he reached to the window dividing back from front and slid it open a little further.

'I can't say as I understand the game you lot are playing, I don't,' he said. 'In my time I've seen a lot of things go on in the back of my cab, but what I've seen and heard tonight is not nothing I've ever seen or been involved in before. But I reckon these people are playing hard. They're playing hard to win something, believe me. And they're playing with you.

'But you don't seem to take what's happening to you very seriously at all. You'd best wake up, love, that's all I can say. They're using you for some rather nasty business, if you ask me. It's not right, and that *is* all I've got to say.'

Genetta stared, dumbfounded, as he finished his speech. The streetlamp outside leant a cosy ambience to the interior of the cab, and the warm confined space and the driver's frank and paternal tone made her think seriously about his words.

'So, what would you do in my situation?' she asked softly, and suddenly felt like crying. Suddenly she felt very tired and in need of an affectionate hug.

'Well, if you're asking me, I'd get out of this "scene", if that's what you call it.'

'What if I told you I've tried, but can't?' she asked. 'Every time I make a break for it, someone I thought I knew and trusted drags me back in.'

'Seems like a dangerous game, love, like I said,' he said

pensively. 'I can't believe that a year ago, even six months ago or whenever, you'd be getting as involved as you obviously are now. To me, and over the years I've learnt to be a pretty good judge, you don't fit. You just seem too nice to be involved with people like that. I'd guess something's gone a bit wrong for you. Looks to me like you're giving up your – well, assuming things were normal for you before you got tangled up in this mess – you're giving up your life.'

He shrugged again. 'But, as I say, they've paid me well, so who am I to judge?'

Genetta looked into his dark eyes. They were bottomless orbs of black – knowing and kind. It had been a long time since someone looked at her in such a compassionate way.

'I – I really don't know how any of this happened to me,' she admitted, and her voice caught in her throat with the sob that was still there.

'It doesn't really matter what has already happened,' he observed sagely. 'What matters is that you get out of this mistaken life right now. And stay out of it in future... that's if you really want to, of course. I can only tell you as I see it.'

Genetta looked at him through tears that blurred her vision and nodded. 'I've got business to take care of here first, though,' she said. 'I know where we are and I know what to do.' She did not elaborate further, but what she had to do was also what Jack wanted her to do.

The driver nodded in a barely discernable way and turned back around in his seat. She could tell from his attitude that he knew she was going to do something more involving this bizarre alternative lifestyle she'd become embroiled in, and she actually felt sad and guilty for letting him down.

'Oh, this sad, submissive soul of mine,' she muttered, as she swiped at a tear with her knuckle. Then she said to him, a little louder, 'I've just got to do this; doing this will help me break with the past.' For some reason she felt she owed the cabbie, a virtual stranger, an explanation. 'I have to see the person who initiated me into this world.'

'Fine,' he responded abruptly, his unexpected warmth suddenly gone again. 'I was paid to wait. I'll be here when you're finished providing your services.'

Genetta wanted to say more, to try and justify her behaviour, but what had to be done had to be done.

Feeling empty and alone, she leaned forward and pulled at the door handle. It clicked back and she shoved against the heavy door, which gave way and let her out. 'I won't be too long… really,' she said to the driver, but he had pulled his flat cap down over his eyes, slunk down in his seat with his stout arms folded across the expanse of his generous paunch, and was feigning sleep. 'Fine,' Genetta said, slamming the back door shut.

She tugged the coat more tightly around herself, and when she reached for the belt she was grateful to find it still hung from the loops. Pulling it snug around her waist, she tied it into a fast knot, making sure that the leather strap was flat all the way around. She was going to see Marie, therefore appearance mattered.

With steady steps and a deep breath she began to walk along the pavement. Marie's door was easy to spot; it was the only sober, sombre one on the street of brightly painted entrances and welcoming façades. It was navy blue with white mitred blocks edging it. Genetta could hardly forget its imposing, distanced look, even though she had been permitted to see it only a few times – the few times Marie actually took her out somewhere.

As she walked ever closer to that doorway, Genetta's trepidation dissipated and she began to get more and more angry. Memories from the weeks she had spent with Marie started to cross her mind, even after all the time and the effort she had put into forgetting.

The night Marie had left her at the club was her first experience of group sex. Her first experience with the rough desires of men when they were given their lead and permitted to act all together and one after another to get what they wanted. Had Jack put her in a similar situation tonight so she would remember by association how difficult that was, to be set free by Marie? Was she to remember what it was like to have the collar taken from her throat? Did Jack want her to remember how truly and completely naked she felt then, plus call to her mind the fact that she had not been able to find another owner to take her and keep her since then? It was an extremely cruel exercise, if that's what he was doing. But it was also highly effective because Genetta was responding in a way that would make sure she cut all ties to Marie, here and now.

The dark blue door through which she had passed months ago – and through which she had never completely re-emerged – stood imposingly at the top of a set of stone steps. And there it was.

Genetta stopped and looked up at it. Resting in the shadow thrown by the grand stone arch above it, the dark door was as mysterious as the rites of passage that Genetta had gone through beyond it. And Marie's controlling character was apparent even out here, in the calm of the street. For the first time, Genetta noticed a small surveillance camera perched in the corner of the ornate stone façade.

Good, she thought, Marie would be expecting her.

Emboldened by that thought, Genetta marched up the half-dozen steps and pounded on the door with the large metal knocker.

Marie opened the door in the middle of one of the knocker's strikes, and Genetta was surprised by the way the woman drew back, apparently startled.

'Hello Marie,' she said.

'Genetta. What are you doing here?'

'I've come to thank you,' Genetta said, pleased that her voice was not betraying the misgivings she really felt.

Marie looked her up and down. 'You look in a bit of a state,' she said. 'Not what I expect when you come calling on me.'

Genetta looked down at herself, then met Marie's gaze steadily. 'The state I'm in is precisely what I want to thank you for.'

Marie leaned against the doorframe. Clearly she wasn't going to ask Genetta in. 'But it's late, and you're a dishevelled mess, Genetta Macleod.'

'This is the same sort of mess that you let me get into when you left me that night in the club.'

Marie did not look particularly interested. 'I left you there with those men because you seemed to need it,' she asserted. 'You seemed to really want out of our relationship. I assumed that because you obviously wanted to get involved with a man again, so I gave you many from which to make your choice. Unfortunately, while their cocks might have fit you perfectly, you didn't fit their requirements.

'And so you're still alone, I see.' She looked pointedly at Genetta's bare throat, devoid of collar or chain.

'That's not the only reason I'm upset,' Genetta said to her former owner. 'I'm angry because of the way you brought me into your circle of perverts, and then left me – alone. I've had nowhere to turn, and no one to approach for guidance since you set me free.'

'Being set free was your own fault, Gen,' the woman said breezily. 'You know that if you had performed better—'

'There was no way to perform better,' Genetta objected. 'There's no way I ever would have been able to live up to your demands, Marie, and you know that. You were looking for a way to get rid of me, from the beating over Kate's Daniel right through to the very night you let me be a mattress for all those men in the club. All that time, you were looking to move on.'

'I would have been happy to train you, Genetta—'

'No, you didn't want to train me,' Genetta insisted adamantly. 'You wanted a girl who was already completely a lesbian; like that Claudia, or Rory. One of that type. It didn't matter to you that to please you I was more than willing to try to be a lesbian, though. You wanted me to conquer my instincts without any help from you, while you rode me about everything else.'

Marie looked at her, seemingly surprised, and then began laughing. 'Where on earth did this all come from?' she asked. 'I wanted a girl who was already gay? Sweetheart, recruitment is part of the fun for me – and you know that. I had no problems with the fact that you didn't think of yourself as a lesbian. The only problem was that when you had a chance to be around a man, you went for it. You were a dyke whenever it was convenient for you, my dear – never when it was good for me. That's really why I had to get rid of you.'

‘That non-incident with Daniel was one lonely time in all our weeks together!’ Genetta said passionately. ‘You took me so far along in my puppy training, and then left me in the lurch. I’ve felt totally lost… and alone.’

‘Those are simply the rules of the game, Genetta. You failed to play properly, and you lost.’

Genetta glared at Marie, then lifted her chin defiantly. ‘So, would you like to go down on me now?’ she challenged. ‘Right here and now. Would you like that?’

She pulled open the bottom half of the coat and offered herself to the dominatrix who had once held her in her thrall. ‘How would that taste to you tonight, do you think?’ Genetta taunted. ‘After all the rampant men I’ve been with?’

Marie stared at her, totally unflappable. ‘I always knew you were a pig, Genetta,’ she said calmly.

‘I would rather be a pig for any stranger than take your wannabe, latex cock ever again, Marie. But I’m done. I’m done obeying Jack Adams, and I’m done with you and the past. This chapter in my life is over, once and for all.’

‘You’ll be sorry if you think you can walk away from all that’s happened to you, Genetta Macleod,’ Marie warned. ‘I promise you; you’ll be quite, quite sorry.’

Without another word Genetta turned and walked back down the six steps that took her to the pavement. She did not hear Marie’s door close, nor did she look around to see if the woman was still watching her. She simply walked along the pavement, towards the cab that still stood waiting by the kerb.

Chapter Twelve

Genetta emerged from the underground and paced determinedly towards the office building. Her heels clicked positively on the paving slabs beneath her feet. The sound made her feel professional and efficient. Today was the day when she would break a sales record – or at least achieve her own personal best. The lackadaisical ways of her past were behind her. No more would she shirk difficult phone calls or customers. She would work harder, faster, set up more holidays for more people, sell more air fares – she would be the best in the office and then, after she had worked her way up to stellar recommendations, she would find a way to get the hell out of there – away from Marie and Tracey and the rest of them. Only when she no longer worked for Mowbray's could she really say that she'd left this part of her life behind her.

Crossing the small office car park, the one restricted for use by the company's directors, she stopped for a moment and stared up at the sky. It looked like being a beautiful day. She walked to the back door and pulled the heavy steel barrier open.

The general hubbub of office noises floated through the air along the short corridor, greeting her with their reminder of work to be done.

She opened the interior sepia door that separated the corridor from the open plan office space, and as she swung confidently around the corner partition and passed the first cubicle group, things went significantly quiet.

As she walked deeper into Mowbray's office and continued past the desks of other girls who handled the phones, people stopped talking. Keyboards went silent. Genetta frowned and noticed that some of the girls were turning to look at her, and others were avoiding making any eye contact, apparently suddenly very interested in the various papers on their desks. All in all, her newfound confidence was quickly being eroded by the sudden hush that fell over the scene.

And by the time she reached her desk she just sensed she was going to see something bad, but she was not prepared for the vast nothingness that greeted her eyes.

Ibiza and Jamaica were gone. Her posters were gone. The wall was sheer blank white where they used to be.

Those posters had graced Genetta's wall from the day she had come to work in this office. More than simply being bright and colourful and cheerful, they had indicated her place in the bland office space – but now they were gone.

Their removal was a statement.

And there was only one person brash enough and cruel enough to do such a thing.

Genetta did not bother sitting at her desk. There was no point. The inevitable call would come soon enough, either an announcement over the intercom system that connected all the workers to the queen bee, or a private internal ring on the phone.

The chosen method of summons was the latter. The phone beeped and its little red light winked, and coolly, determined to maintain an air of self-control, Genetta answered it.

'Hello...' she said clearly, although her throat felt dry and tight.

'Genetta, this is Marie,' came the woman's stern voice, confirming the inevitable. 'I want to see you in my office, immediately. I believe you know why.'

Genetta replaced the receiver, noticing how her clammy palm clouded the plastic's sheen, without saying a word in response.

She stood, positioned the chair neatly into the leg space of her desk, and then walked towards the door leading to the managers' offices.

'Nothing to say about any of this, Tracey?' she asked the back of the girl as she passed.

No answer was forthcoming, not even an acknowledgement that her question had been heard, just a momentary hesitation in Tracey's fingers over her keyboard, but Genetta would not have stopped to listen to her anyway. She was on her way to have it out with Marie again, and this time it would be different because there was obviously nothing left for Genetta to lose.

Into Marie's office she went, without knocking. She had not been in here alone with Marie since those after-work hours when Marie had initially seduced her. For a second, Genetta wondered how the Mowbray dynasty would like it if they knew what use their plush office furnishings were being put to.

But she pushed the thought out of mind. What was happening right now required her full attention. As she closed the door behind her and turned to face her former mistress and now former office manager, Genetta realised that what transpired in the next few minutes could influence her entire future.

'You know what's happening,' Marie said tersely, 'but we don't need to get into all that. Clear out your desk and be gone within the hour.'

'I have to say, I'm a bit disappointed, Marie,' Genetta said, trying to strike a conciliatory tone that both she and Marie knew was false. 'When you and I ended our little fling, you said it wouldn't impact upon my employment status here. You said my job wouldn't suffer, that nothing in my professional life was at stake and that you had played with a lot of girls who'd worked for you, without your personal life ever interfering.'

'Did I really say all that?' the woman mused. 'How magnanimous of me. However, I must point out, that was when I thought I knew something about you, Genetta. Somewhat disappointingly, though, your behaviour lately has shown that I actually knew very little about you, which annoys me, because I am not normally wrong. And so the terms of our agreements have changed as time has gone by.'

'You've liked me less and less, haven't you?' Genetta said.

'You've shown sides of yourself that aren't... shall we say... particularly submissive. And that's what I haven't liked, Genetta.

'And I think you'll find,' Marie continued, crossing her legs with a seductive whisper of silk stockings, 'that very few other masters – or mistresses, for that matter – will care for it either.'

'But that's for me to find out myself, I believe,' Genetta said, turning slightly and reaching for the door handle. 'And if you've finished, I think I'll be going now.'

'Wait, Genetta,' said the woman, uncrossing her legs and leaning forward, her forearms on the uncluttered desktop. 'There's one other issue I want to settle with you.'

She turned around and looked at Marie. 'And whatever

could that be?'

'Quite simply, I want you to meet your replacement.' Marie turned her eyes towards the door to her left.

Genetta followed her gaze to the same door, the door that led to where Marie's secretary worked. She looked uncertainly at it for a moment, and then said, 'No, really, you've made everything perfectly clear, I know where I stand and I'll be going now.'

'Claudia, come out here please,' Marie called, ignoring Genetta's statement of intent, watching Genetta, closely reading her reaction.

Genetta cringed – Claudia. She knew that Marie had taken Claudia as her new slave, but to have it thrown in her face like this still hurt.

'In what way is she my replacement?' she asked. 'Just in your bed, or on the end of your leash, as well?'

'In every way,' Marie answered her.

'Fine, Marie – I really don't care, to be honest. I take it I won't be getting a glowing reference from you, I can see that much. And that's really all that interests me now. So I'll go and clear my desk, box up my life at Mowbray's and go home.'

'Oh no, it's not that easy, Gen,' Marie said, pushed back from the desk, rose gracefully and made her way to the main office door, where Genetta stood gripping the handle. She was very close to Genetta now, and as she looked her in the eye, she slowly turned the key in the lock and removed it. 'I want you to see how a good slave behaves.'

It was at this point exactly when Claudia appeared.

'Just the three of us,' Genetta sneered. 'How very cosy.'

Marie pulled Claudia to her, and then pushed her hand up the back of her new girlfriend's skirt. 'No panties, just silky softness – how lovely.'

'What's the point in doing all of this, Marie?' Genetta asked.

'I'm trying to communicate to you, my dear, that you are disposable. Whatever happens to you in your life after today, bear in mind that you are completely replaceable. No master or mistress gets so involved with a slave that you can expect to get away with anything you want. You're going to have to be a better-behaved girl, Genetta. I gave you the benefit of this speech once before, but I'm hoping it sinks in this time.'

'Thanks so much for looking after my welfare,' Genetta answered sarcastically and rolled her eyes. 'But now could you unlock the door, please?'

'Fine, Genetta, have it your way. I'd be willing to take you on as my pupil again, but you'd have to serve under Claudia now.'

Genetta looked closely at Marie's expression; it was one of cunning and slight amusement, and Genetta did not like its portent one little bit.

'Thanks but no thanks,' she replied. 'I want to leave, and I want to leave now.'

Marie, still fondling the purring Claudia, produced the key to the door for Genetta, offering it on her open palm. 'Very well, if it's what you really want,' she said with condescending arrogance.

Genetta did not hesitate for a second, grabbed the proffered key and unlocked the door, turned on her heel, and holding her back straight and chin high, walked out of Marie's office.

She paced down the corridor, back to what was her desk, passing Tracey once again, but this time she had nothing to say to her former friend. She opened the top draw of the desk and began to remove her possessions. Some of the pens she had bought herself scattered and rolled over the top of the desk and fell to the floor behind it. Undaunted and beyond caring, Genetta got down on her hands and knees and crawled into the leg space under her desk to retrieve them, but when she re-emerged her temper was simmering.

'Actually, Trace,' she said, standing up and walking to the cubicle where her former friend appeared to still be engrossed by her work, 'all of this *is* really beginning to piss me off.'

Tracey continued to simply look at her computer screen.

'Talk to me,' Genetta demanded.

'What do you want me to say?' Tracey asked crossly. 'And what could you possibly have to say to me?'

'What's the matter with you?' Genetta asked, startled by her friend's aggressive demeanour. 'You know, Trace, when I got involved with Marie, she told me that in no way would our little relationship have any adverse consequences for my job. I guess I never really believed her – I mean, if things went wrong between us, how could they not detract from our professional relationship? But honestly, I never would have thought things between her and me would cause any problems between us. I thought we were actually friends.'

'How could I be friends with someone like you?' Tracey said hurtfully.

'Someone like me?' Genetta was shocked at what she was hearing. 'What the hell do you mean by that?'

Tracey stopped her intermittent typing and spun around on her seat to face Genetta. 'I mean someone like you – a poor submissive, a bad slave. A person who doesn't respond to proper training. In the culture we are involved in – that you tried to be a part of – decorum and grounding are paramount. You behaved abominably at Marie's; arriving there like you did and accusing her of all sorts of nasty things. I can't possibly be a friend of yours. Being friends with you would violate everything I believe in.'

'Tracey speaks the truth,' sounded Marie from the other side of Tracey's cubicle. 'What's fascinating, Gen, is your irreverence, your rude mouth and your bad attitude. To think that after everything you've been through you still insist on behaving this way. I would say that you require yet more training, but you don't respond to it. You're a pig-headed, stubborn brat.'

'And as for what Marie said concerning your involvement with her not reflecting on your job,' Tracey said, 'she probably presumed that a trained submissive – or a supposedly trained submissive – would never behave so abominably.'

'It looks like she needs more work, doesn't it, Tracey?' Marie said. 'Even though we are probably sure of a negative outcome.'

'Definitely,' Tracey concurred, as Genetta began to feel threatened.

Suddenly somebody grabbed her arms from behind. She struggled in pursuit of freedom, and turned to see her assailant. It was Claudia. 'I got turned on, having Marie play with me in front of you,' she said. 'Perhaps a wrestling match will give us both the release we need.'

'I'm not playing this sick game with you bitches any more,' Genetta announced, again trying to wrestle free from Claudia's grasp. 'I'm a devotee of men only these days.'

'You're a devotee of punishment, I think,' Marie observed. 'And Claudia is just the sort to give it to you.

She's been learning a thing or two from me.'

With that, Claudia dragged Genetta backwards by the shoulders, making her lose her footing. Tracey jumped forward to grab the prisoner's ankles, and together the two female captors swung Genetta around and lifted her until her bottom was on the edge of the desk.

Claudia lost her grip on Genetta from behind, but during the struggle she managed to get hold of her wrists and held her tight once again. Genetta kicked out, but Claudia leaned forward and pushed her back, pinning her to the desktop.

Genetta glanced around and caught Tracey's eye. She opened her mouth to speak, but Tracey began herself. 'Paul and I want nothing more to do with you,' she hissed vehemently. 'Do you know that? I've decided that you're no longer to be a friend of ours. Oh, and by the way, you are scrubbed from the club's books – I thought I'd let you know that, too.'

'You've decided that you and Paul are finished with me, have you?' Genetta challenged. 'I'd like to take your word for that, Trace, but I think Paul has other ideas.'

'What are you talking about? He's submissive to me in regard to such matters.'

'Oh, right, well explain to me why he paid a little visit recently. He came over with Jack the other night and the two of them took me on quite a trip around town. It was the same night I showed up at Marie's.' Delighted with her comments, which clearly unsettled Tracey, Genetta quickly pressed on. 'So I might be a "bad slave" to you miserable tops, but to your precious boyfriend I was an awful lot of fun, believe me. And will be again, I shouldn't wonder.'

Claudia grabbed Genetta's hair and dragged her head to

one side in an effort of intimidation. 'Shut it,' she ordered, before twisting her hips in order to get between the pinned girl's legs. Genetta did not care any more what they physically did to her; she *really* wanted to win the mental game.

Claudia fumbled around on the desk, searching for something with her free hand as she kept her eyes glued to Genetta's face. Genetta concentrated on making a beatific expression appear; the last thing she wanted was for Claudia, Marie's minion, to know that she felt afraid or in her power in any way.

Genetta stared deep into Claudia's eyes, defying her to invade her peace of mind. But just then a look of triumph came over Claudia and she stood up, tugging something from the desktop. Still with her hair in Claudia's clasped hand, Genetta wrenched her head around and tried to see what her tormentor had grabbed.

It was the mouse. Genetta sighed. She felt the whole experience was becoming absurd.

Without further ado, Claudia grabbed the hem of Genetta's skirt and began to push it upwards. Tracey helped, and they got it up to Genetta's bottom. Genetta refused to co-operate. She knew what sick trick Claudia had in mind, and she was not going to give them the satisfaction of thinking she was in to their games.

Claudia placed her hand under Genetta's skirt, still holding the mouse. Genetta looked down and saw the cord trailing out from between her legs, still attached to the computer that had been the centre of Tracey's work. She tried to close her legs to prevent Claudia from having her fun, but it was not possible, at least not with Claudia's hips wedged between her knees and Tracey doing her damndest to hold on tight, as well.

The rounded edge of the mouse nudged at the underside of Genetta's panties. It tickled her, brushing through the delicate material against her pubic hair, and she involuntarily relaxed a little, causing her thighs to part ever so slightly. Claudia clearly sensed this and took the initiative to push the mouse inside Genetta's panties.

The smooth edge nudged downwards against her sex, and Genetta sighed and ground her hips to greet it. She decided to enjoy being masturbated, refusing to consider how she was being violated right there, in front of all the girls in the office.

She knew they were all gathering around. She heard the wheels of their chairs rolling back on the plastic insets underneath their desks. Their high heels tapped on the plastic and made scuffing noises on the industrial carpeting. They were watching Claudia have her wicked way with her.

They were now all involved.

They were all Marie's girls, Genetta thought, as Claudia shoved the broad mouse up into her, soon leaving only the cord hanging out of Genetta's sex. She then grabbed the cord and pulled, slowly. Genetta felt the mouse emerge from her body. The mouse was now completely out of her, but caught between her body and the cotton crotch of her panties.

She kept her head thrown back, secretly revelling in this little game of workplace submission, determined not to feel defeated.

'Enough,' Marie announced, and Genetta knew that the woman was finished only because Genetta was clearly not going to be intimidated. 'Let her go. I never want to see her in this building again.'

Claudia bowed her head and pulled the mouse from

Genetta's panties. Tracey and Claudia both took their hands off her, but allowed their fingertips to glide over her as if they longed to touch her for a while longer. The rest of the girls drifted away and Genetta waited for their sounds to recede before she sat up and straightened her clothes with as much dignity as she could muster.

Soon they were all gone – scurried back to their places like rats caught exploring a new part of a maze.

She slipped down from the desk, moved back to hers and opened another drawer. Grabbing its handle and pulling it off its rails, she threw it against the nearest wall, where her posters used to hang. She then proceeded to do the same with each remaining draw in turn. She dumped the contents of them all onto the floor, and began to kick things out of her way as she walked towards the exit.

Feeling abused and exploited, she left the building for what she hoped was the last time, and prayed that she could now begin to get her life back together.

Chapter Thirteen

Genetta looked around her flat, paying close attention to the contemporary furnishings she had bought on credit. Their polished veneer glared back at her, bright in the lights she had turned on throughout her living space. She had chosen each one of those, as well, for ambience, focal points and task lighting, just as the interior decorating manuals had told her to do. But now the expense that each one represented was getting on Genetta's nerves, along with the quarter sawn oak furniture, and the maple cabinets in the kitchen, and the American arts and crafts style table that graced the living room, with the four chairs, each one costing more than the dining table itself. All of it was pound after pound after pence, gone from her savings account and wallet. And all, each and every thing, still demanding money to be paid on it.

Genetta flopped into a chair she had bought for comfort more than looks. It was a good thing it cradled her body so sumptuously because she felt like she needed to be babied for a while.

She had lost her job, and Marie would never provide her with a decent reference in her hunt for another one. It was as if the last three years of her working life did not even exist. How could she account for all of that time to a prospective employer?

She leaned forward and picked up the folder containing all her certification as a travel agent. These papers were useless without the job experience she had garnered working at Mowbray's. How had this happened? It had all seemed like a pervy but maybe fun sexual game at the beginning. How had it ended with her losing her job, staring over the chasm into severe debt, and possibly even a few missed mortgage repayments away from losing her home?

Genetta had severe problems.

She had to talk to someone who could influence Marie, she thought. If she could only get a good letter of reference from her, just a few short paragraphs on her reliability and performance as an employee, then she could leave the entire sorry episode behind her once and for all. But who on earth could influence Marie that way?

There was not very much hope. Now that Genetta no longer worked at Mowbray's, and if Tracey was right and her name really had been scrubbed from the club, then she had no way to get to Marie; not through anyone else and not by herself. She certainly did not think it would be wise to show up on the woman's doorstep again.

They all belonged to the club; Marie, her new love Claudia, Tracey, Paul, and Jack Adams. They were all players in that scene. Especially Jack Adams.

Genetta nibbled her lip as she pondered, turning over the thoughts racing through her mind.

Jack Adams had been her first contact in the scene. Yes, she had worked well for Marie before that time, but Marie had never made any moves on her until Jack came into play. It was like Genetta's contact with him had set everything else into motion.

Jack was the key. If she was going to find a way out of this mess, she had to find a way to Jack Adams.

And yes, they were all members of the club. So there was only one thing to do…

As the cabbie took the ten-pound note, Genetta paused, hand outstretched. The words and advice of the last cabdriver she had come into contact with came back to her, and she knew he was right. This was a nasty business. What she was about to confront was a nasty business, involving nasty people. But sometimes the only way to get out of something was to go a bit deeper into it.

Well, that was the strategy she had to go with right now, anyway.

Mentally she apologised to that good-hearted cabbie as she crossed the street, running with small steps because of the tight skirt she wore. It constricted her thighs nicely, and between it and the high heels she wore, it was an effective bondage outfit.

The door looked as uninviting and intimidating as ever, but Genetta could not let her reservations thwart her now.

She had a job to do.

Once again she was in pursuit of a master, only this time she could not stop until she had found Jack Adams. He was the only one who could help her with the Marie problem and the job problem and all her other problems. And once he had exerted his influence over Marie to help Genetta get sorted, then, Genetta swore to herself, then, she was through with all of this.

Leaning into the heavy door she opened it and stepped inside. As it swung shut behind her its blackened glass filtered all the light from out on the street.

The doorman glanced up at her, and then looked again. It seemed to register with him who she was; as if at first he could not believe that she would actually come back here. And when the realisation sunk home with him, he began shaking his head.

'No, no, no,' he intoned. 'Absolutely not… no way,

Genetta… I can't let you in here.'

'Why not?' she asked sweetly. 'You've done me some favours before.'

'Before, you were at least in semi-good graces with the established members of this club. But now, I'm verboten to let you anywhere near the premises. If certain members were to see you out here I'd be in the same bloody shape as you are when they sacked me. So no, Genetta, you've got to leave.'

'But I have real reasons to be here,' she insisted. 'If I don't talk to Jack Adams—'

'I'm sure that to you your reasons are of paramount importance,' he cut in. 'But I'm telling you that it's not possible for me to let you in. You're *persona non grata*. I know you know it, so you don't require any more explanation from me. Just leave, please.'

'I know you like me,' she persisted.

'Of course, I like you,' he admitted, his voice relaying his exasperation. 'What is there not to like, really? But that doesn't alter the fact that as the doorman and guardian of the entrance to this club, I've got a job to do.'

'I'm sorry that I never learnt your name,' she pushed onwards. 'I'm really sorry.'

'And there's no point to your knowing it now. I really doubt that you and I will ever cross paths again.' He stood up and walked around his desk to her.

'Leaving your little *point d'appui*?' Genetta asked. 'I thought you weren't fully comfortable unless you were sitting on your wee throne back there, guarding the gates of heaven.'

Standing before her, he smiled. 'Let's go,' he said, good-naturedly. 'Come on, shift. Get out of here before I have to get you out of here myself.'

'Mmm, wouldn't you just love to get a little rough with me, though?' she taunted.

'I'd like to get more than a little rough with you, Genetta,' he disclosed, 'and I suppose that anything you and I did on our own time would be just that – on our own time. But right now I'm on the club's time. And there are only so many more ways that I'm going to tell you to get lost.'

Not to be deterred, Genetta reached out and boldly let her fingertips trail over his crotch, and was immediately rewarded with the feel of his cock responding. It stirred beneath her palm, uncoiling and stiffening. Encouraged, Genetta purposefully slid her hand lower and cupped his balls, encompassing their heavy softness.

He groaned quietly, and she knew she was getting through to him.

'What do you want more than anything?' she asked him, whispering seductively. 'I'll give it to you if you just let me inside for one last time.'

'But I have duties to perform,' he grunted, his voice slightly strained.

'And you have duties to take care of for your own body, too,' she tantalised. 'Your own desires and pleasures, for example. They should be foremost on your mind.'

He looked up tormentedly, gazing over her head without seeing as the warm feminine hand coaxed and teased. Genetta studied his strong jaw, admiring the masculinity of his features and thinking that she could, indeed, do anything he wanted her to do.

'All right,' he said finally, unable to resist what she was doing to him any longer. 'I'm going to sit down at the desk again. You get under it, and you suck my cock. Then we'll see about calling Jack Adams to come and get you. Just this once, mind; if he doesn't want to see you or he's busy or whatever, then too bad. Because no matter the outcome for you, your relationship with this club and its clientele is over after this evening. Okay?'

Genetta nodded; she was getting closer to her objective.

'Okay,' he said, sealing the deal, 'come on then.'

Genetta followed him around the desk, but stayed back a little as he sat on his armless chair.

'Come on then,' he repeated, his excitement evident, 'get on your knees and do what I told you.'

Obediently, Genetta slipped down onto all fours and moved gracefully beneath the desk, and without further delay, the doorman grabbed the zip of his trousers and eagerly tugged it down. Genetta nuzzled his crotch, but he pushed her face away with the back of his hand and fished his own turgid cock out of his underwear.

He stroked it a few times while Genetta licked the single eye with the tip of her tongue. She slipped down to the underside of the shaft and paid some attention to the spot right at the base of his glans, where the helmet curved into its smooth bell shape. He groaned softly and she suckled the head of his dick between her lips, holding it gently while her tongue worked all around the top.

He let his breath out, hissing between his teeth, and then wrapped a fist in her hair. Genetta let him drag her head to one side, and there she licked up and down his ever-hardening erection. It felt as if there was a steel rod encased within the velvety flesh.

He pulled her head to the other side, and Genetta turned her face to his cock and gave it the same treatment on that side, being sure that every lick, kiss and touch of her lips was symmetrical to what she had already given him.

'Take it into your throat,' he said in a broken, gravely

voice.

He let go of her hair and Genetta centred herself between his thighs. She could feel his muscles tightening already – this was going to be fairly quick. And that would be fine.

She took the head of his cock in her mouth again, and then gripped his shaft at the base. She slid her palm up and down a few times, gripping his prick with a steady pressure in her fist. He moaned, a tortured sound, and Genetta buried his meat in her mouth at the same time that she took her hand away.

With her own heavy breathing and the chair creaking under his bottom, she could not hear much else. Genetta concentrated on giving him pleasure and bringing the situation between them to fruition – that was all she had on her mind. Once she brought him off, she would be a step closer to getting into contact with Jack Adams and working with him to finally put an end to all of this. Yes, she thought as her head bobbed up and down at a constant rhythm, driving the doorman on towards his orgasm, yes, she would have to service Jack in the same way, about that there was no doubt. But soon, she told herself, she would be on her way out of this life, on her way back towards finding some sort of normality.

Thoughts of solving her problems clouded her mind as her breathing became heavier. Perspiration dampened her brow and she felt a drop roll down the bridge of her nose, buried as it was intermittently in the doorman's trousers and dark pubic hair. But as he stiffened and came, Genetta suddenly had the horrible feeling that the more she fought to free herself from their clutches, the more entrapped she was actually becoming.

Chapter Fourteen

Jack Adams parked his car, turned off the ignition, and turned to look at Genetta. The darkness of the night made his eyes nothing more than impenetrable shadows.

'I'll open your door,' he said, heightening her awareness of the uncomfortable metal cuffs locked to her wrists. 'You will get out without a sound, and we are going up to your flat. Don't do anything to draw attention to us. Do you understand?'

She nodded.

'Good.' He reached down for his briefcase, which was at her feet in the shadows of the foot-well. Then he got out, walked smoothly around the front of the car, and opened her door. With a little difficulty, and a little assistance from him, Genetta managed to get out too, and together they entered the entrance hall of her building.

He took her purse, slung as it was over her shoulder, and searched for her key ring.

'Which one is it?' he asked, as he held the keys up in the half-light. 'Nod when I have it.'

Genetta watched him hold each key and did as he ordered when he got to the one that opened her front door – the same key she had fumbled with weeks before, the first time she was ever with him.

Once inside he closed and locked the door, placed his case on the telephone table in the darkened hall, and dropped her keys into it.

'Do your arms hurt?' he asked, nothing much more

than an indefinable bulk in the semi-darkness of the small hall.

She nodded.

'Shame, because I rather like you with you arms behind your back like that; it throws my favourite parts of you into relief,' Jack said. He moved closer and she stole a glance at his face, just to see where he was looking. She could tell he was admiring her curves, his attention captured by her breasts.

'Very good,' he said, 'very good indeed for my viewing pleasure,' and Genetta noted the approval in his voice. 'I'm going to take the cuffs off now, as you're being such a good girl.'

She turned and offered her arms to him as best she could and waited as he reached into the pocket of his trousers to get the tiny key. With the cuffs unlocked and removed Genetta rubbed her wrists to get the circulation back.

He turned her round again, looked deep into her eyes, and then, taking by the arm, led her through to the lounge. 'Now Genetta,' he said firmly, 'sit down.' He gestured towards one of her chairs.

Still rubbing her wrists she walked to it and sat down primly. She was not sure what to expect and it seemed a good idea to mind her manners and try to be attentive while not anticipating what he wanted – she knew that Jack hated anticipation; he liked to be fully in control.

She did not cross her legs, but held her knees and ankles together and kept her feet flat on the floor. Jack said nothing and Genetta did not look at him. She simply rested her hands on her knees, her back straight. Other than sitting properly and quietly, she acted as if no one else were in the room with her. Her job was to react, not create the action.

Jack had his case with him. He put it on the spare chair, all the while staring at Genetta. She peeped at him, but tried to keep her gaze lowered as much as possible, and he did not seem to mind her thieving glances. Genetta actually thought she caught a little smile playing about the corners of his mouth as he did so, but she did not look long enough to be sure.

'Lift your legs and place them over the arms of the chair,' he said, moving closer to her.

Genetta wondered what he was up to, but taking a deep breath, she obediently leaned back into the comfortable piece of furniture, lifted her legs and did as he ordered, the tight skirt almost proving an obstacle to his demands, but inching even further up her thighs to allow her to comply, giving him a glimpse of her white panties, nestled snugly over her soft mound.

But Jack was in no hurry; he was clearly savouring every moment. He walked behind the chair, and gently touched her hair. Genetta purred a little and pushed her head against his fingers, but then they were gone and she could only sense him – watching her.

The silence had Genetta holding her breath, and then he moved again, leant down and looked into her face with an unsettling intensity. His stare pinned her where she sat, mesmerising her with its utter self-belief.

A hand touched her thigh and Genetta gasped, startled by the suddenness of the movement, but she maintained the eye contact, knowing that's what he wanted – what was expected.

His eyes seemed to glow from the shadows cast over them – consuming her.

Fingers touched her lips, which sensually peeled open,

following his unspoken command as a knot of excitement gripped her.

Jack pressed, and Genetta eased her head back and closed her eyes as his fingers probed her mouth.

'Look at me, Genetta,' he told her, his other hand moving gently on her inner thigh, slowly circling and moving higher. 'Look at me while I'm touching you.'

Slowly, she opened her eyes again until her gaze met his. He was watching her closely, as if waiting for some kind of reaction – but she was not sure how to react. Did she enjoy what he was doing? Or did it unsettle her?

'Not so good,' Jack said after a long tense moment, and she knew he was dissatisfied that she had not yet completely let down her guard against him.

He withdrew his fingers from her mouth and straightened up, looming over her where she slumped in the chair, her legs parted, feeling extremely vulnerable and exposed. Dispassionately he looked down upon her, then bent again and ran his thumb over her cheekbone.

Genetta nearly melted to feel him touching her so gently. She shut her eyes to let him know she was converging all her power of thought on his touches – paying them the utmost respect.

His fingertips traced the delicate shape of her ear and sank into her hair. 'Lovely,' he said quietly, as though to himself. 'Very lovely...'

Genetta made no attempt to reply; it was still advisable to keep quiet and enjoy being the centre of Jack's attentions.

He ran his thumb over her cheekbone again, down over her upper lip, and then her lower lip as he continued on his way to her chin. 'I love your lips,' he said, and leaned in very close to her. Genetta sat motionless as he brushed his own lips across hers, barely touching her, causing her to tremble with exhilaration.

She closed her eyes, expecting him to kiss her passionately – wanting him to kiss her passionately. But he didn't; he slowly slid his lips down to her throat, his fingers following their path. Then as his lips rose again and nuzzled just beneath her ear and he inhaled deeply the fragrance of her hair and perfume, his fingers continued on their downward exploration and cupped her breasts. Genetta took a deep breath, filling her lungs, eagerly offering their fullness to his hands.

He caressed and kneaded through her delicate blouse and bra, his strong and demanding hands possessing her. He pinched her erect nipples, and with her legs spread wide over the arms of the chair, Genetta was sure he would take her soon. She wanted desperately to ask him to, but she had no permission to talk.

But then his lips and hands left her. She sighed, her body luxuriating in and missing the sensations his touch had evoked. Then she dreamily opened her eyes and looked up at him.

'Open your blouse and undo your bra,' he said, and with instant deference Genetta unbuttoned the buttons of her top and allowed it to fall open, exposing her lacy white bra and shadowy cleavage. Her bra was clasped tightly shut at the front, something Jack seemed to expect, and so without having to move from her submissive position she was able to unclip it for him and slowly ease the soft cups apart, revealing her flesh to his avaricious eyes.

He studied her for long silent minutes, a look of satisfaction evident in his usually inscrutable expression. She looked up at him, barely daring to move, awaiting his next move.

Without bending Jack reached out and cupped her nearest breast. He sunk his fingers into her flesh, much harder than was necessary. Genetta gasped and her head dropped back against the chair. He began kneading her breasts in earnest, pinching her nipples, causing her to moan softly. He touched her body as if it did not belong to her; he touched her as if she belonged to him.

Jack captured her nipple between thumb and forefinger and Genetta looked down to watch. He rolled it between them, clearly enjoying the spectacle of her pink tip between his fingers, under his control.

Genetta groaned and writhed a little in the chair, pushing her breasts up towards him, revelling in the feel of his hands clamped to them. But then he let go, and with enviable ease of movement, in total control of himself, let alone Genetta, he knelt between her thighs.

Without considering the consequences of such a bold reaction, she reached down to join his fingers as they touched her sex, traced the outline of her through the damp white of her panties. She looked down to see him easing his face closer. Then he hooked a finger beneath the elastic, pulled the cotton aside, and stroked her moist labia.

Genetta pulled the soft pad of skin over her clitoris's hood up and held it tight against her pelvic bone, exposing her sensitive button to him if he wanted it.

And he did. Jack accepted the offer, leaned into the V that Genetta's legs presented for him, and took her clit between his lips. He sucked it into his mouth and expertly rubbed the tip of his tongue up and down its underside.

Genetta moaned and arched her back in response. Could he make her love and obey him, just by treating her body like this? Anything was possible. She moved her hands and placed them on the back of his head. But she applied no pressure – that would be disrespectful. Instead, she simply felt his movements as he vigorously ate her.

She felt his fingers rhythmically squeezing her thighs, and then she groaned loudly as he pressed a thumb against her sex, joining his active tongue.

'This is very good,' he murmured, lifting his mouth away from her, and Genetta, smiling, opened her eyes to look down at him. He smiled at her, and then stood up and went back to his case. Genetta watched him retrieving something from it for a moment, then rested her head back once more and closed her eyes, feeling too relaxed to open them again when she sensed him standing before her. She was doing this for herself. She was taking one last trip through a submissive night in order to finally free herself of this world and everything it stood for.

'Ah, so beautiful...' Jack mumbled, sounding very pleased with her, with the way the encounter was developing. Genetta relaxed more and more into the comforting chair, her breathing slowing as she enjoyed the aura of calm his dominating presence was draping over her.

Then there was a soft click and something flashed. Her eyes snapped open. Jack was indeed in front of her – holding a digital camera.

'No...' Genetta began.

'I told you about not talking, Genetta,' he said, 'and I expect you to adhere to my wishes.'

'I'm sorry, Jack, but I—'

'Be quiet,' he insisted calmly, lifting the camera and taking another series of shots, moving slightly from one side to the other, varying the images.

'I know why you called me to the club tonight,

Genetta,' he said as he worked. 'You want me to rescue you. You've been under the influence of Marie and her cronies for too long, and you need me to help you. And so I came. You called and I came.

'That means only one thing, Genetta; you belong to me now. These pictures,' he nodded at the camera he still held, 'I'll send them to everyone you know should you refuse to accept that you are mine now; after all, I've still got your address book, remember?'

He held up a hand, silencing her instinctive protest before she could let herself down again by speaking without thinking or permission.

'Oh yes, that's what I'll do, Genetta, believe me,' he went on. 'You will accept what I am saying – that from this moment you belong to me – otherwise I will have no other choice but to send these images to your friends and family. The film wouldn't work, because of the anonymity of the hood, but any shots I take tonight will do very nicely.'

He paused for a moment, amusement dancing in his eyes as he proudly surveyed her, looking utterly mouth-watering as she lay back on the chair, her clothes awry, offering tantalising glimpses of her body; her blouse and bra hanging open, her skirt rucked tightly up around the tops of her parted thighs, offering a glimpse of her white panties.

'You will be my lovely domestic servant and sexual slave,' he continued. 'I will keep you. I am your keeper, Genetta.'

He put the camera down and moved close to her side again, his legs touching the arm of the chair. Genetta looked up at him, not knowing how she felt. He had known all the while what she was thinking; that he would help her get away from Marie and the others. How could she have been so stupid? What could possibly have made him give her a lift out of their way of life if there was nothing in it for him?

But then, Genetta thought, maybe she did it all because she wanted to get back to him. Perhaps her subconscious arranged the encounter because she wanted to be kept down. Maybe this was all there was for her…

Jack Adams was stroking her hair, and for the first time she noticed the telltale bulge in his trousers, so close to her flushed face. With a secret surge of excitement, she watched his free hand move to his belt buckle. He said no more, and obediently, neither did she. The only sounds inside the darkened room were their combined breathing.

Mesmerised, Genetta watched the belt fall apart, and his hand move to the zip of his immaculate trousers. With his other hand he still stroked her hair, smoothing the fringe away from her brow, but her eyes were fixed on the fingers that slowly lowered his zipper.

'Open your mouth, Genetta,' he said, his voice at last betraying some emotion, and she knew that she was his.

Chapter Fifteen

'This is where you're going to stay,' Jack announced. It was the following morning and the night of photography was over, and now Genetta was left feeling humbled, because Jack had then taken her to his car and driven her to his house. She felt strange, too, walking around naked in front of the man, in his home.

He threw open the door to a room as if he were leading his slave into a beautiful harem designed to suit her every whim and need. Based on his grandiose action, Genetta had actually expected something when she walked into the room.

But its effect was less than she had hoped.

It was a tiny affair. The bed was so small it looked more like a bench than a proper place to get some sleep. With a rounded metal top and spindles going down, it was a bed-like shelf underneath two side-by-side windows. The windows were shut tight and dark wood blinds were drawn closed over them, completely eliminating any natural light from outside.

Beside the cot was a small chest of drawers, but the only decorative effect was a pair of sconces hanging from the wall. When she looked more closely at them, she could see they held real candles. As for lighting, there was one small lamp next to the bed, which gave off very little light, casting gloomy shadows around the tiny room.

'Am I meant to stay here… all the time?' she asked.

'All the time,' Jack said with one emphatic nod.

She walked a little further into the room. Jack brushed past her and went to a narrow doorway. He turned the carved doorknob and she peeked into a bathroom that was just as tiny as the bedroom, but clad with startlingly white tiles and bathed in bright light.

'All yours,' Jack said.

'It – it's a bit like a dungeon,' Genetta said doubtfully.

'Close enough,' he said. 'Close enough.'

Two weeks later Genetta lay on the cot, watching the candlelight dancing on the wall opposite.

She rolled onto her back, and noticed that something new hung under the sconces. Manacles. They had not been there when she drifted off to sleep earlier. Were they there as a treat – as a special surprise?

Jack must have hung them there while she had been sleeping, and she remembered his evident excitement whilst discussing such a toy for suspending the women he planned on bringing to her cell. His plan, he had said, was for the wax from the candles to drip down on his new whore's hands and arms when he so desired. It would serve to intensify their torment.

Genetta closed her eyes again.

She had gone from a tentative to a total submissive, prepared to accept and revel in whatever Jack decided to perpetrate – or have perpetrated by others – upon her.

The garment she wore was made of gauzy material, which had a sheen to it and shimmered in the candlelight.

The door swung open, and natural light from the hallway poured in. Quickly Genetta sat up on the bed and pulled the sheet up to cover her breasts in a self-protective gesture, and with one hand she half-covered her eyes from the sudden brightness cast upon her.

The glare behind the people in the doorway prevented her from recognising them straightaway, although she knew that one of them would be Jack. Recently when he would come into her room he always asked her about her welfare. This time however, he said nothing.

Instead, he just closed the door behind him and his companion. Genetta looked closely, trying to discern the lady's identity, but as her eyes recovered from the shock of the invasive brighter light, she still did not recognise her.

'My little slave, I know you would like to know who is joining us this evening,' Jack intoned, and Genetta could tell that he was enjoying his masterly role. 'But it is best if you two stay mostly anonymous to one another.' He indicated the girl with him. 'For this evening, this is Portia,' he told Genetta. 'Her dominant lent her to us for a few hours.'

Jack approached the cot, reached out to Genetta and played with her hair a little, before letting his thumb trace her jaw line.

'I am afraid I'll not be touching you tonight, my dear slave. This will be a hard lesson for you to endure, but you've got to learn how to watch me when I'm dominating someone else.'

Genetta took a deep breath, and ignoring her submissive and slave-like tendencies, she decided to speak up and say what she felt she had to.

'S-sir, might I make an observation?' she tentatively enquired.

Jack raised an eyebrow, surprised by the boldness of her request.

'If you must,' he answered sternly.

'You haven't paid me so much attention lately…'

He gazed down upon her for a few seconds, and just when Genetta was wishing she had not spoken up, he laughed spitefully – a reaction that unsettled her. Clearly her observation was not as important to him as she had hoped – or as important to him as it was to her.

But soon he stopped laughing.

'Then it will do you good to see me give my attention to someone else,' he answered. 'It will further remind you of your true place here. Now, first things first. Get off the bed and let Portia lie down with me.'

Genetta obeyed.

Jack took her place and motioned for Portia to approach. As she slowly sashayed towards him, moving provocatively, Genetta could tell she had not totally given herself over to slavery. She was the type of female Genetta used to be, and led the life she no longer craved. She had found her role in life now.

As Genetta observed the developing scene, Jack's attention was totally focussed on her, but when he spoke she knew it was not to her. He was addressing his new toy, but looking for its affects on Genetta's face.

'Suck my cock,' he ordered.

Portia dropped onto the bed, her knees positioned on either side of Jack's, her legs spread wide over his. Genetta watched with jealous interest as she unzipped his trousers and began to take his semi-hard cock out.

'In the top drawer,' he said to Genetta, pointing at the small unit, 'you'll find a nice little butt-plug I put in there earlier, when you were asleep.' She did as she was told and turned around, holding it for him to see. By now Portia was slowly licking the head of his turgid prick, but Jack's attention was still fixed on Genetta.

'Turn around,' he ordered, 'bend over, and insert it.'

When she turned and bent to show him her cleft, the gown she wore rode up her thighs and exposed what he wanted to see. She then reached around and inserted the butt-plug into herself.

'Is that all right, sir,' she asked, 'the way I've done it for you?'

'Yes,' Jack answered casually, as though barely aware of the girl's mouth and tongue working over his erection. Portia's head was bobbing up and down and she was sucking on his length for all she was worth. The sight made Genetta feel that familiar yearning in her pussy that only contact with a man could resolve. But for now, she stood obediently still.

'Stand in the corner,' Jack gasped, Portia's efforts gradually getting to him. His head dropped back momentarily, then he lifted it again to speak to Genetta as she moved.

'Pull up your dress,' he groaned, 'and rub your breasts.'

Staring at her owner, Genetta teasingly pulled the shimmering cloth up the front of her body. She took the hem in her teeth and ran her fingers around the curves of her breasts. This was becoming enjoyable. It had been a long time since she had the opportunity to seduce a man, especially Jack.

Genetta caught the nipple on each breast between thumb and forefinger. But she had not been told to indulge herself too much, so she shut her mind off from any self-induced lust as she looked at her master and began rolling her fleshy tips back and forth.

Jack pushed his hands down on the back of Portia's head, holding her in place. Then he began pumping his hips up and down underneath her. 'More, I need to fuck your face more,' he said, and pushed her off him completely. She rolled onto her side on the narrow bed, and Jack situated himself in front of her face and balanced his knees on the very edge.

Genetta watched the other female move her head until her mouth was in line with Jack's rampantly hard prick. She took it between her lips, and his hips again began pumping and she enjoyed watching him fuck the mouth of another girl. Taking, as he always did, exactly what he wanted.

Continuing to play with herself, she pinched her nipples even harder and tightened her bottom around the butt-plug. She let herself enjoy the sight of her master going at another girl's face and mouth.

Genetta then realised that she was submitting to his wishes and not to her own desires – but she did submit.

It took nearly a month after that evening, but eventually Jack began giving Genetta the sexual attention she craved.

While bathing her master, Genetta ran the sponge down his back. He flexed his shoulders and she washed across them, carefully caressing him. She admired his frame and watched the water run off his skin in rivulets, like rain trickling down a window during a storm. Inside the small bathroom all was peaceful, and she felt content.

'What do you really want, Genetta?' he said out of nowhere, and a little surprised by the unexpected question, she pondered an answer.

'What do you want?' Jack asked again, leaning back in the bath. 'Out of all things on this earth, what do you really wish for?'

'To serve you well,' she said. It was the obvious answer, and the one she thought he would expect.

'No, no,' Jack replied, but the smile he wore relaxed

her. 'There must be something you want besides submitting to me. That was never like you before, and I suspect that somewhere inside, you're still the Genetta I met in the club so many weeks ago.'

'Do you mean something I want now or something I used to want?' she asked, wringing out the sponge with a hard squeeze.

Jack ran a hand down her bare forearm and took her hand in his. 'Something you have always wanted. The thing that you covet most in this world.'

'I guess it's too late now, but what I really wanted, for a long time, was to have my own business. You know, to be the boss of my own travel agency.'

'Like Marie?' he asked, smiling teasingly.

Genetta shook her head and pulled her hand away from him, then sat down on the chair next to the bath. She crossed her legs and looked at her master carefully. With this dominant she was allowed, no, she was encouraged to look him in the eye. He liked her to meet him as an intellectual equal.

'No, not like Marie,' she said. 'Not at all; she's merely a manager, for one thing.'

'But you have to walk before you can run,' Jack said philosophically.

'Yes, I know that. But I always wanted to have my own agency. That's all.'

Jack ran a wet hand across his chest, leaving a streak of bubbles. She looked at it and licked her lips, idly hoping he would invite her into the warm relaxing water with him. But he did not.

'Do you know what I think, Gen?' He did not wait for her response before going on. 'I think that perhaps you got involved with Marie and all of this in the first place because you wanted to find a way to advance yourself professionally.'

'No, that's not it... that's not it at all,' she denied, and that truly had never been her motivation.

'I know it's not ethical,' he said, 'to want to sleep your way to the top, but did you ever stop and think that perhaps that's what you were doing?'

'Really, sir, my problem could be that I never stop and think about anything.' There, she had let him know how little she considered her actions when she got involved with him, and Marie, and this entire lot.

'Hmm,' he mused, 'then why did you do it? Why did you get involved with us and take on the role of a submissive?'

Genetta glanced down at the floor, then back towards his soapy chest. 'I guess I did it because it felt good,' she said, and her admission was met by a prolonged silence.

Sensing that the conversation was over, Genetta stood up and went to get him a towel. The water sloshed around in the bath, making her look back. Jack was sitting up to turn on the jet streams, and as the motor hummed to life he settled back against the flowing water. 'Gen,' he said, 'you've not been out for a long time, and I must admit that I've been indulging myself with you. But you've been bearing up very well, so as a little reward, would you like to go out somewhere this evening?'

'Whatever you want, sir,' she said, placing the towel on the chair where he liked it for his convenience. She paused for a moment, waiting to see if he would give her another order or ask her to do something for his comfort, but he didn't, so she took his silence as a dismissal, walked into the bedroom, and sat on the edge of his bed.

About a quarter of an hour went by, during which time

she let her mind wander over nothing in particular. Oddly, this mental vacuity was one of the areas of satisfaction Genetta found in the life she currently led. There was little to think about save for serving Jack, regardless of the time, day or night.

She had no need to think about anything else but her master. Her basic needs were taken care of, and nothing else was any of her business. The only problem she had was making sure that she was serving him appropriately and living up to the standard of submission that would make him happy. It seemed… yes, on most days, most times, it seemed good enough for her. Serving her master was enough.

Jack then emerged from the bathroom. He was towelling himself off, but Genetta jumped up and stepped forward to take it from his hands and perform the task for him.

'No, no, it's okay; for once I want you to do something for yourself,' he said. 'I meant what I said in the bath. It's about time you and I went out together. Do you want to?'

'Whatever pleases you, sir,' she said.

'Very good,' he said. 'All right then, I'm going to get ready, and then I'll select your clothes for you.'

Genetta could smell the freshness of the soap on his body as he laid the outfit on her small bed.

Trying to seem like she wasn't paying too much attention to what he had chosen, she eyed it from where she was. The dress looked plain and demure. It was black cotton, judging by the texture she could see in the dim light. It had a scalloped and embroidered scoop neck. Next to it, Jack had laid a pair of suntan-coloured hold-up stockings and black heeled shoes.

'We'll brush your hair back smoothly and you will wear very little make-up,' he said. 'Perhaps some foundation, if that makes you feel comfortable.' He looked at her closely in the candlelight that spread constantly from the sconces. It was as if he was awaiting a reaction, but she did not give him one.

She pulled her shift off and dropped it on the bed, next to the wardrobe he had picked out for her. She then sat down, picked up one of the stockings, and carefully rolled it up in her hands. Gently, she placed her foot into it – this was the first time in a very, very long time that she had worn anything on her feet, and the feeling of the material sliding over her skin was exquisite. Genetta closed her eyes in order to savour it more fully, and then smoothed the second stocking on too.

She slipped into the dress. It fitted her perfectly and came down to just above her knees, and then she stood up to ease her feet into the snugly fitting shoes.

Jack moved towards her, holding the brush he had picked up from the chest of drawers where all of her belongings were. Genetta turned around in front of him.

The brush traced the contour of her head, pulling and straightening her lustrous hair at the back. It ran through the long tresses that had grown unhindered since she came to live here. Her hair was now down to past her shoulders.

Genetta, absorbed in the moment, remembered how it felt good to be treated so well.

'I think I have changed my mind,' he whispered, 'we don't need to go anywhere tonight.' He started to rub the back of her neck with one hand as he continued to use the brush with the other. She sensed, even craved, that he wanted to spank her bottom with it, to lay sharp hard smacks across her buttocks as he took her from behind.

'No, sir,' she said softly, 'not if you don't want to.'

'I would far rather we two be alone together, all night,' Jack said. 'Would you like that, my dear?'

'I would like that, sir,' she answered truthfully. She swallowed, and then ventured to voice the next thought that crossed her mind. 'I would like that for evermore.'

It was not to be quite happily ever after, but as Jack moved up beside her and pulled her down on the bed, Genetta trusted that he knew what she meant.

Lost in the world that Jack had brought her into, that Marie had infused in her, that Tracey and Paul had augmented, to which Jack now provided the finishing touches – Genetta, the once young-woman-about-town was lost. Only a slave remained.

And still, to this day, Genetta submits.

More exciting titles available from Chimera

1-901388-23-9	Latin Submission	*Barton*
1-901388-19-0	Destroying Angel	*Hastings*
1-901388-26-3	Selina's Submission	*Lewis*
1-901388-29-8	Betty Serves the Master	*Tanner*
1-901388-31-X	A Kept Woman	*Grayson*
1-901388-32-8	Milady's Quest	*Beaufort*
1-901388-33-6	Slave Hunt	*Shannon*
1-901388-34-4*	Shadows of Torment	*McLachlan*
1-901388-35-2*	Star Slave	*Dere*
1-901388-37-9*	Punishment Exercise	*Benedict*
1-901388-38-7*	The CP Sex Files	*Asquith*
1-901388-39-5*	Susie Learns the Hard Way	*Quine*
1-901388-40-9*	Domination Inc.	*Leather*
1-901388-42-5*	Sophie & the Circle of Slavery	*Culber*
1-901388-11-5*	Space Captive	*Hughes*
1-901388-41-7*	Bride of the Revolution	*Amber*
1-901388-44-1*	Vesta – Painworld	*Pope*
1-901388-45-X*	The Slaves of New York	*Hughes*
1-901388-46-8*	Rough Justice	*Hastings*
1-901388-47-6*	Perfect Slave Abroad	*Bell*
1-901388-48-4*	Whip Hands	*Hazel*
1-901388-50-6*	Slave of Darkness	*Lewis*
1-901388-49-2*	Rectory of Correction	*Virosa*
1-901388-51-4*	Savage Bonds	*Beaufort*
1-901388-52-2*	Darkest Fantasies	*Raines*
1-901388-53-0*	Wages of Sin	*Benedict*
1-901388-54-9*	Love Slave	*Wakelin*
1-901388-56-5*	Susie Follows Orders	*Quine*
1-901388-55-7*	Slave to Cabal	*McLachlan*
1-901388-57-3*	Forbidden Fantasies	*Gerrard*
1-901388-58-1*	Chain Reaction	*Pope*
1-901388-60-3*	Sister Murdock's House of Correction	*Angelo*
1-901388-61-1*	Moonspawn	*McLachlan*
1-901388-59-X*	The Bridle Path	*Eden*
1-901388-62-X*	Ruled by the Rod	*Rawlings*
1-901388-63-8*	Of Pain and Delight	*Stone*

1-901388-65-4*	The Collector	*Steel*
1-901388-66-2*	Prisoners of Passion	*Dere*
1-901388-67-0*	Sweet Submission	*Anderssen*
1-901388-69-7*	Rachael's Training	*Ward*
1-901388-71-9*	Learning to Crawl	*Argus*
1-901388-36-0*	Out of Her Depth	*Challis*
1-901388-68-9*	Moonslave	*McLachlan*
1-901388-72-7*	Nordic Bound	*Morgan*
1-901388-27-1*	A Strict Seduction	*del Rey*
1-901388-80-8*	Cauldron of Fear	*Pope*
1-901388-74-3*	In Too Deep	*Beaufort*
1-901388-73-5*	Managing Mrs Burton	*Aspen*
1-901388-75-1*	Lucy	*Culber*
1-901388-77-8*	The Piano Teacher	*Elliot*
1-901388-25-5*	Afghan Bound	*Morgan*
1-901388-76-X*	Sinful Seduction	*Benedict*
1-901388-70-0*	Babala's Correction	*Amber*
1-901388-06-9*	Schooling Sylvia	*Beaufort*
1-901388-78-6*	Thorns	*Scott*
1-901388-79-4*	Indecent Intent	*Amber*
1-903931-00-2*	Thorsday Night	*Pita*
1-903931-01-0*	Teena Thyme	*Pope*
1-903931-02-9*	Servants of the Cane	*Ashton*
1-903931-04-5*	Captured by Charybdis	*McLachlan*
1-903931-03-7*	Forever Chained	*Beaufort*
1-903931-05-3*	In Service	*Challis*
1-903931-06-1*	Bridled Lust	*Pope*

* * *

Sales and Distribution in the USA and Canada

LPC Group
1436 West Randolph Street
Chicago
IL 60607
(800) 626 4330

* * *

B3